Write Where We Are

WriteOn Joliet Fourth Annual Anthology 2020

By WriteOn Joliet

Cover art by Mauverneen (Maureen) Blevins

2

WriteOn Joliet anthology 2020 contributors: Denise M. Baran-Unland, Holly Coop, Steven James Cordin, Jessica Harris, Tom Hernandez, S. Houk, Lindsay Lake, James Moore, James Pressler, Colleen H. Robbins, Duanne Walton, Katie Ward

I want a page -
a white page and black ink -
and to shake the hands,
hands, and hands
of everyone who made: writing.
The thin line of ink,
the nib, the nub,
the inkwell and desk
where we carve our names.

S. Houk

ABOUT WRITEON JOLIET

WriteOn started as WriteOn Minooka, co-founded by Denise M. Baran-Unland and Kristina Skaggs. Our members come from all over the southern suburbs.

Some have self-published or have been traditionally published. Others are still exploring their writing options and interests. Regardless of our place in the writing world, WriteOn welcomes everyone looking to write, read and grow.

WriteOn Joliet is a welcoming, diverse group of writers of varied skills, interests and experience. The group includes professional journalists, fiction novelists, bloggers, screenwriters, musicians and poets.

We promise a safe, comfortable and supportive atmosphere to share your work, and constructive feedback so that everyone can benefit from our shared knowledge.

WriteOn is a dues-paying organization. The first visit is free.

For more information, visit writeonJoliet.com.

TABLE OF CONTENTS

BEHIND CLOSED DOORS

By Holly Coop

Atop a snow-white throne

Shielded by ignorance
The heart of a nation was shown
Brutality wore its crown
People were beat down

Victims fled in silence
Toward the light of a new day
Sheltered by the dark cold ground
Where hope would lead the way

Clanking of shackles
Ring echoes across the land
While hearts beat
Throbbing, blood soaked blisters
The only warmth to aching feet

Those with golden hearts
Pretending not to see
Secretly waved from the shadows
To the brave who chose to flee

Offered a path
They searched for land
Where they would be safe
Be free
Believing that someday they would see

One nation in unity
Tunnels became their towns
Stories of Fathers and Mothers
Passed down by sisters and brothers
Their legacy would live on
And for others who dared to dream
Hope would lift the chiseled frowns
Of a people beaten down

Humanity would be left for dead
The sight of its tarnished crown
Would forever be a thorn in its head

The haunted lies of a past
Filled with violence, hate, anger
Brutal and heinous acts
Unforgivable facts
God's people will never be free
From the division beget
From the scars left
By their tainted history

We must free ourselves and give up the sins of the past
And *in love* offer up our sorrow,
If we are ever to see a unified world of tomorrow

For human beings will only be truly free
When we all live in unity
When hearts flowing with the same red blood
Beat in harmony
We are all created from one
Universal Source of Love
And when we die

Our sins won't lie
We will ALL be judged

CARDBOARD HOUSES

By Holly Coop

A prayer...

Give me the willingness and courage

To right the wrongs I have done – from my lack of *doing*

Bring about a change in me – of mind and heart renewing

Move my limbs to perform actions that are good

There are so many without roof, water - food!

Lend to me Your resources to help shelter, clothe, feed

Everyone deserves *at least* the **basic** human needs!

Bend my ear to hear those that cry in their silence day and night

We must construct a solution to eradicate this nation's homeless plight

Crowds hurrying past – their busy pace they keep

Yet no one to hear the mute voices - of the many mouths to feed

People flooding designer stores - in and out they walk

No one there to notice *cardboard houses* - lining city blocks

To those who pass - on their *own* beaten path - futilely making paces

May their hearts and blind eyes be opened to see

With empathy the faces! - Staring blankly in defeat -

From the cut out windows - of cardboard houses lining streets -

We are humanity...in need

CELEBRITY CRUSHED

By Lindsay Lake

He had the eyes; a blue like no other.
His alabaster skin so white, his jaw
more structured than my life and his dimpled
chin recessed into a heartbroken vulnerability.
Muscles, every kind and shape adorn his massive
chest. His divinely shaped thighs brought grown
men to tears. His lips alone could launch one
thousand ships. Alpha male. They want him.
They wanted him. Touch his hair! Touch his hair!
That silky long stream of moist green grass,
lush-fresh and alive. But she swatted him like
a fly and his broken body oozed and
squirmed and twisted on the swatter until
she knocked him to infinity.

CHILDREN OF LIGHT

By Jessica Harris

A man walked down the road, his figure casting a long shadow before him. The sun was still at its peak, but the intensity had waned. He wore a deep-cowl cloak and large tinted aviator goggles made from whatever he could find, staying covered from head to foot. A thin scarf pulled tightly against the flesh covered the bottom half of his face. He carried a few knives in holsters and two in his high leather boots.

The area was desolate but not empty. Instead, like all the times before, a fearful silence greeted him; a tension in the air of those hiding, lying in wait for the man and his shadow to pass. Only once on his travels did he turn and could almost hear the collective sigh of relief at his passing. Perhaps he had imagined it then—no, he was sure he had heard it.

He thought he heard a sound and stopped. It was to his momentary surprise that an infant, still wrapped tightly, rolled from the protective shadow of a nearby building and stopped in his shadow. The fearful silence intensified to bated breath. The only thing that broke it was the helpless wailing of the baby so recently torn from its mother's breast.

"Madam, come claim your child." There was no response. Instead the quiet seemed to almost stifle the child's cries. Wind beat against tin roofs and moaned through wooden crossbeams creating an unearthly chorus.

"Madam," the man repeated. He need not raise his voice as it carried heavy and well through the entire town that he knew watched. "Claim your child before I lose my patience and expose him to the light." There was still nothing.

He waited. Just when he believed no one would come and he should be on his way, he saw a soft flush of movement off to his left. He saw her then, eyes wide and terrified as they peeked out behind a heavily curtained door. She couldn't have been more than nineteen or twenty years of age. Tears streaked her face as she edged out slowly. The man regarded her casually as if the woman brought him no satisfaction or disregard – and she didn't.

She moved slowly like an animal knowingly in the gaze of its predator. She never broke eye contact with him as she continued forward, only looking at the infant to ensure her own hands did not leave the safety of the shadows. She dragged the infant out of the man's shadow and into the more comforting dark of the buildings before quickly picking it up and cradling it, shushing it to quiet it. The man watched her a moment as if satisfying himself of her safety before moving on.

"WAIT!" The voice cried out behind him, making him stop. He'd been through many hamlets in the years and never had anyone called to him. He turned. She remained there, looking at him with the hatred he'd come to expect, but also a fiery determination he rarely saw anymore. It reminded him of himself all those years ago.

"My brothers are just behind me and will end you if you do anything so foolish as to come closer," she warned.

The man chuckled. She had no brothers, that much he knew. Based on the hardened square of her shoulders he suspected she was alone and used to being so.

"You called me, madam?"

"Why did you protect my child?" she asked. "Nearly all of your kind would have exposed him the instant he came to view."

"'My kind,' are not mine. I am one of you, though cursed out of the shadows and into the light."

"*Liar!*" She hissed and he expected it.

"If saving your son was not proof enough, then there's nothing I can say. I must away now to find a place to rest. I'm tired and in desperate need of respite." He turned.

"Wait!" He heard again. It was softer this time. "Please...wait. At sundown join me here." She indicated the shanty that was her home.

Grateful tears filled the man's eyes, blessedly invisible behind his mask. After six years of wandering, he would finally have the ability to connect to another unmarked person. Foolish, perhaps, but it was the first time someone asked him to wait. The man sat in front of the house.

He waited.

The darkness settled when she returned. He hadn't moved as the sun slunk down and the artificial lights began flickering and buzzing to light. He didn't move as the hamlet sprung to life: the first hesitant sounds of motion, then with increased flurry and enthusiasm. People would give him a wide berth, often with ill-hidden distain. Still, he didn't move.

She appeared then, the infant undoubtedly in the arms of caretakers. It was the first time he moved, her slightly nervous expression reflected in his wide goggles.

"Do you eat food?" she said by way of greeting.

"Of course."

"You have a surprisingly pleasant voice. Come on."

She jerked her head and disappeared into the yawning darkness of her shanty door. He got up slowly and followed. Inside were four other women, all of whom shied away from him. The babe was still missing and this was not lost on him. Despite her somewhat warm welcome, she didn't trust him enough to have him in the home with her child.

"Stop," the woman he followed chided the other girls.

They quieted themselves but did not move from their huddled mass in the corner. They each held a small bowl of food.

15

Nothing was offered to him, nor did he ask. Instead, his stomach gave a painful growl. The woman came back with a bowl of her own, as well as an empty one.

"Here," she said, handing it to the first woman. "Put a little of your food in it, then you a little of yours and so on so we can feed our guest."

But the first shook her head adamantly while the woman next to her pretended to be oblivious, picking at her food and staring at the ground ahead of her.

"Damnit, Charlie, show a little compassion!"

"Absolutely not," she said and with that she turned so her back was to the woman, who grunted.

Without further hesitation she handed him her own food. He was going to refuse, but it'd been three days since he'd eaten last; he didn't know the last time he ate actual meat. He pulled his scarf down and began to eat. The other women watched him, ashamed, as he finished the entire thing.

"Thank you."

"Nimue," a man's voice said from the door. He quickly covered his face again with his scarf. "It's been brought to my attention that you've admitted one of the Light; is this true?"

"Not in the way you think," she defended. She squared her shoulders in a way that implied she would not be intimidated. "He's one of us, though touched by the light."

"I heard him myself. You believe him?"

"He saved my son – no creature of the Light would have done it."

The man simply grunted before turning his attention to him.

"You got a name, wanderer?"

"I've had several over as many years; that one suits me best, I think."

"What does? I would not suggest you try me."

"Wanderer."

16

"As you wish. Come with me to the meeting of elders."

Wanderer had attended many of these meetings and knew exactly what to expect.

"Wait! Nicolas, hold on – "

The man grabbed her roughly by the arms and shook her slightly.

"You have just threatened us all with your act of bravado! Don't you dare –" Nicolas choked as Wanderer threw him off of Nimue and held him by the throat.

"I may be a sojourner, but the woman has been kind and I will therefore see to her while I am here. Touch her again at my displeasure."

Nicolas shoved him off.

"Fool," he spat and walked out.

Assessing that Nimue was alright, Wanderer followed. Nicolas led him to a centralized building, octagon in shape and built intentionally shorter than all the others. He knew it was so that the taller buildings on all other sides would cast a shadow over it during nearly all points of the day except for Execution time: high noon. Unless this place was so very different than the one he had lived and loved in, there were networks of tunnels built under all the shanties, used only in emergencies and at night when they could be open and the children could come out. During the day, the children were put to sleep down there while the adults guarded from the shadows.

Heard even from outside was the sound of heated debate; voices swelled and rolled like waves, the occasional word or phrase being sprayed high above the rest before the cacophony settled into a foam of white noise. Wanderer knew what all the arguing was about.

It was about him.

As soon as they stepped in, the room instantly quieted. Benches were built along three of the four walls, the door being the only spot in the fourth wall. Nicolas sat at the edge of one of the benches; the other spots occupied by the men that had been currently debating. These were the elders of this community, the ones that handled food rations, support, and guards for the citizens.

He was not invited to sit so he remained standing. Candles burned gently in the room, allowing enough light to see but still leaving the bulk of the space in darkness – darkness and silence as the elders stared at him, all too afraid or unsure to speak.

"You have saved one of our own today. We thank you for it," said a man who sat in the center-most of the room in the only chair. He grunted as he rose to his feet and with no hesitation the others did as well. They remained standing in appreciation for a moment before sitting again. "However, you must understand the danger and complication your presence here offers us."

"I do."

"Then we will ask you to be on your way."

"I will be happy to leave," Wanderer said. "But I humbly ask for a chance to rest. I have been traveling for years with no respite and I have injuries that must be attended to. I will stay no longer than I need and I will ensure that none of the people of the Light – that you should rightly fear and abhor – appear to you or your people while I'm here."

"And how will you do that?" Another man said; presumably the youngest of the council.

"I will either appear to them as they pass by; in seeing one of their own they will have little reason to believe there's any Unmarked here. I will hide my location so I am not detected or summoned. If the situation calls for more extreme measures…let us hope it will not come to that."

"How do we know we can trust you?" another man said. "We've got family here: women, children."

"You don't."

18

That led to another bout of screaming; some advocating that Wanderer be quickly expelled, others that he be killed, and others that they give him a chance. After a chaotic moment, the leader spoke again.

"You say you have not been tainted by the Light, only cursed to walk in it." Wanderer nodded. "Tell me how this is possible."

For the first time, Wanderer visibly hesitated.

"If I'm to honor your request and save your life in exchange for saving the life of one of ours, I demand to know how it is you can say with such confidence that you will not be bring a hoard of your kind on our heads. I will not assume to take your word on it."

"You are a wise man, Elder," Wanderer said. "But that is a story wracked with pain and misery, and one I'd rather not engage in."

"Your preferences are hardly my concern, son of the Light."

Six years earlier

"I said *stop it*, you cad!" she said giggling.

She slapped him playfully on the chest before pulling him into her embrace and kissing him. The smile still played on his lips as he embraced her, resting his chin on the top of her head.

"Never, my love."

She giggled softly as she buried her face into him, curled up in the cool of the day. She was precious to him – so precious. He'd loved her from afar and never thought such a beautiful creature would notice him. It was to his surprise when he was walking toward the pasture one night that he felt arms grab him suddenly. He turned to strike his assailant but saw it was her, his lovely Phoebe, and his eyes widened in shock as she pressed her tightly closed lips innocently against his. He could only stand frozen as she burned in crimson embarrassment and ran back to the shanty her family dwelled in.

"Oi! Get moving!" A voice jolted him back to the present and he grinned like an idiot the rest of the night. That was so long ago now he couldn't remember how old he'd been: twenty? Twenty one? And she was a girl of hardly eighteen. Now, as they waited for the sun to go down to begin the night's work, they simply enjoyed each other. Their child, a beautiful girl named Bethany, was asleep in her swinging cradle. She was still too young to go to the tunnels with the other children, but for right now she enjoyed napping in the shade.

Something caught his attention; at first he dismissed it as an odd sensation, but when it didn't go away he directed his senses toward what could be the cause. Phoebe had fallen asleep, and her stillness and level breathing allowed him to focus on other sounds: the creaking of the swing crib, the wind rattling against the tin roof and gentle rustle of unknown things blowing down the street. It was then that he was able to pin-point it again: the sound of soft, quiet movement.

He slipped out of bed and quickly dressed, keeping his gaze locked on the window closest to the swing. He slowly inched his way toward it to look and see what it was that was making that noise, all the while avoiding the light. He took a steadying breath. Then another. Then he moved back the wooden shutters standing deeply in the shadow.

The sun was setting now, so this side of the house was blanketed in darkness. Noting that, he stuck his head clear out the window and saw nothing: no movement, to sign of life whatsoever. Chiding himself for being paranoid, he closed the window and turned around only to stand in mute shock as he looked at the figure of a young boy, one knee on the bed above Phoebe's still sleeping form.

The boy had a knife shakily pointed at him. His eyes were wild in panic, but it was no less intense than the fear that gripped his heart and caused his lungs to stop working.

"Food, man!" the youth said – for his voice betrayed his age – "wherever you keep it, bring it out, now!"

"We're a small family, you idiot. Get out of here."

"They always give the families extra," he said with a chuckle that sounded deranged. "The rest of us starve while you guys get as much as you stuff in your fucking face!"

"Get out of my house," he growled again, knowing he could easily disarm the boy but hesitating to do that as he was still above Phoebe.

"Food! I swear I'll cut her!"

He jerked the blade toward her and pressed it on her throat. He saw her eyes were open, though she remained still to not aggravate the boy. Her eyes found him and almost pleaded with him.

"Okay, put the knife away and I'll get it," he said, holding his hands in a placating gesture.

He seriously doubted the boy knew how to use the knife but was afraid he'd hurt Phoebe by dumb luck or accident. He moved slowly toward a jar that was sealed tightly. He picked it up and walked carefully over.

"Open it up," the boy said.

He didn't want to do that; this jar was empty.

"I can't hold it and open it. Put the knife down and we'll see about getting it out of the jar together, eh?"

"I said OPEN IT!"

Everything happened so quickly there was hardly time to breathe. The boy's screaming woke Bethany, who began screaming at the top of her lungs. The boy's head snapped in that direction, so he used the surprise to throw the jar at him. The boy grunted as the heavy ceramic knocked him off balance and he fell backward, but the knife hadn't been moved and Phoebe instantly placed her hand to her neck as she began bleeding. He saw red rivulets streaming beneath her hand and was immediately overcome by anger.

He grabbed the boy and twisted his knife hand as hard as he could as the thief tried to stab him. There was a sickening snap as the wrist was broken and the boy screamed in anger and pain. Bethany began screaming louder and Phoebe instantly went to her, cradling her and holding her tightly.

The sight of both his wife and daughter covered in blood further enraged him and he grabbed the boy bodily off the ground and threw him out the front door.

"NO!" Phoebe cried, instantly recoiling.

There was no light, but it was a dangerous move; opening the door in Light time. He couldn't be expected to reason. He pounced on the boy in the shadow of the house, pinning him down and punching him again and again. The boy's face was bloodied.

The Wanderer grabbed the boy by the throat and began pressing. The boy's eyes bulged out of his head and spit foamed and dribbled in a mad mess. He clawed helplessly against the hands that held him until in a sudden, blinding grip of the last of the day, a cloud moved bathing both the boy's head and the Wanderer's hands in light.

The Wanderer instantly recoiled, even as the boy screamed and then went still. Wanderer began shaking his hands furiously as if that would dislodge the pulsing forms that arched their way over his skin, ending at the wrists which had remained in shadow. The boy's entire head was showing the uniform signs and patterns. In an animalistic cry he got up and ran full-bodied into the light, stripping off his clothes.

"NO!" Wanderer cried, but it was too late.

The boy was completely enveloped. Wanderer watched in mute horror as the boy continued to run and disappeared into the distance. Panic seized him as he headed back into the shanty, careful to hide in shadow.

"Are you okay? What happened?"

"The boy's gone; ran."

She paled.

"He *ran?*"

"I tried to stop him, but he was an animal; screaming and shouting. I couldn't make hide-nor-hair of it." He reached toward her. "Let me see."

He tilted her head back and examined the cut across her throat; it was shallow. If it was kept clean, it shouldn't scar much and should heal well. Wanderer said as much. Her eyes had been wide in panic and she was shaking her head, even as she clutched Bethany tightly and stepped away from him.

"You should be alright, Phoebe."

"It's not me!" She said, pointing at him. "Look! You've been marked!"

He looked at his hands once again to confirm that he hadn't been able to escape his exposure to the light.

"I didn't mean to," he said. "That boy…."

"What are going to do?" she asked.

Tears welled in her eyes as she sat on the bed. He sat next to her. She flinched away from him, but settled back into his arms. That subtle movement, that jerking away, constricted his heart but he understood it and held her for no fault for it.

"We'll keep it a secret for now," he said slowly. "I'll wear gloves or keep my hands hidden."

"How long will we be able to keep that up?"

"Just pray it's long enough," he said.

She sat curled in his arms, only this time it was different. It wasn't the intimate, soft gesture of before, but instead a frightened shock of uncertainty. He was stroking her hair as he allowed his mind to drift on terrible things.

"OW! Stop it, you're hurting me!"

He didn't realize it, but he pinched the back of her head in a strong grip. He willed his hand to release her, but it seemed to have taken a life of its own.

"Let go!"

"I'm trying!" he said.

With an immense amount of strength, he pried his hand back. She was terrified and he was mortified as he willed his hands into submission. They'd been pricking with a strange sensation; micro needle-points stabbing his skin, but as he waited he noticed the sensation lesson, as did the appearance of any mark on his skin.

"Why would you do such a thing?" she demanded.

"I didn't," he said, staring hard at his hands as if some answer was to be found there. He looked at her, pleading for the same and saw only her hurt. "It was as if…I had no control over my hands."

They stared at each other for a long moment and both of them realized the same truth: they wouldn't be able to hide this. He'd have to go in front of the council of elders and that meant he'd be expelled. He'd never see his wife or his daughter again. There was terror in Phoebe's eyes as she rocked a fussing Bethany. Their eyes stayed locked, though they both knew what had to be done.

The night came and everyone whispered about the disappearance of the boy. At first they tried to find him, but word quickly spread from one shanty to the other than he had left in daylight hours and hadn't been seen since. A sense of mourning filled the air as he was just a boy, driven to madness and death by the light.

There was an emergency meeting called by the elders. They met in the center hut, lit only by candlelight. Phoebe and Bethany were allowed in, sitting quietly in a dark corner far to the edge: Phoebe looked terrified of the future ruling while Bethany slept.

Wanderer was driven to his knees and kept his head hung low. The debate rang passionate. Some elders were attempting mercy for him, given that he'd been a valuable member of the community for many years. Besides, they argued, he didn't give into the light as all the others had; didn't that mean he was still of sound mind and judgement? Others considered him a contaminate no matter his history; he was now of the Light and no one of the light could be trusted. Besides, weren't *all* those of the light once valuable members of their community?

There was no end in sight. The Wanderer could only listen in terror as the sway of the elders went first one way, then the other. He was not permitted to speak during this process, so he said nothing.

Phoebe had been the one to report him and promised to speak an impassioned word for his salvation. He'd thrown up the second she left and his body broke down into sweat and tears. He was shaking and pacing like a terrified caged animal. When she collected him and told him she'd walk with him to the hut, he was thankful for her presence and steeled his shoulders against the sense of dread. He needed to be strong for her.

"Silence!" Chief Elder Igor shouted above the din.

After a moment of continued words, the elders returned to their seats and watched with expectation as the final judgement would be cast.

"We have before us a strange case," he said. "And the decision to be reached should not be done hastily or without due consideration. As Chief, the final choice rests with me. Is it true, sir, that you engaged with the lost boy during daylight hours?"

"He attached my family, sir. He –"

"The time for pleading is over. Answer the question." Wanderer hung his head.

"It is sir."

"And is it true that it is the result of this altercation that led you to be Marked by light?"

"It is sir."

"And did you, in the quiet of your home, attack your wife?" The Wanderer hesitated.

"Sir? I'll not ask again."

"In no intention, I assure you."

"And is it true," Elder Conrad interrupted, "that you have yet to succumb to the madness? You are yourself hale and whole?"

"With my whole being sir; I've no desire to go into the light. I fear it as any wise man would."

"And is it true at the time of the attack, you attempted to stop the boy from entering the danger of the light?"

"It is sir."

"And is it true that the boy attempted to enter your house *from outside* during daylight hours?"

"It is sir."

"Well, there you have it!" Elder Conrad said as if a great debate had been settled once and for all.

"It is not so simple as if he was right in what he did," Elder Igor said. "We, each of us, know that if we were forced into the same detestable situation that we would, men of us all, defend our families to our dying breath. The question is if he will expose us to the light, to bring them upon us and destroy us all?"

"I've no intention to do so, sir."

"Your 'intentions' are of little interest to me – it's only the realty of your actions." He sat down heavily. "It seems that while you are of hale and hearty mind now, how long before your spirit breaks? How long before all of us are subjected to the light or killed? Or will it ever happen? This is unknown. No one has ever contacted the light and not been driven mad."

He rubbed his eyes in an exhausted manner. The room waited with baited breath and until he stood up and heavily and slammed his staff down.

"Hear this, the judgement of your elders: As you have not yet succumbed –" The Wanderer felt his spirits lift, but tried to temper the hope that welled up inside of him. "And are not yet a threat to this community, we acknowledge you." The other elders rose and gave him praise before sitting down. "And, as you have protected not just this community but also the man that attempted to harm your wife and child, we acknowledge you." Again, the elders rose and praised him before sitting down.

"However, despite your words of assurance, I have to weigh the fact that you brought harm to your own wife – if even outside of your control." The Wanderer's stomach dropped. "Therefore, the final word of Judgement is this: You are to be stripped naked and tethered to the Shadowless Post. If you succumb to the light, you will be forever removed from us. If you remain in your facilities – as you have shown yourself capable – you will be brought back into our community, in which time we will sentence you punishment for both the assault of your wife and the driving out of the boy."

"Elder Igor!" Phoebe beseeched.

"Silence now! The Elders have spoken."

Men the Wanderer grew up with: Stephen, with the wisp of a beard that he still couldn't grow and Alfred, with his ginger hair and muscular frame– grabbed him. Wanderer wanted to fight. Every instinct told him he should demand that this not be done, scream in rage for the injustice, fight the hands that held him and run to embrace Phoebe and Bethany for perhaps the last time – all of these died with the firm grip of the men.

He was already treated suspiciously. If he acted out, they may just kill him on the spot and then there will be no chance. But to be tied to the Shadowless Post was not a chance either.

"My love," Phoebe ran to him with tears in her eyes. "My darling! I didn't know! I...please tell me what to do!" She had stopped in front of him, blocking the men from leaving.

"Phoebe, step aside," Alfred said not unkindly.

"Shut it, twerp!" she snapped. "The Elders haven't forbidden it so I'll have a word with my husband!"

"Peace, Phoebe," Wanderer said. "Take care of yourself. Everything will be okay."

"How can you say that?" she said, aghast. "Should I raise our daughter alone?"

"Fighting will ruin any chance of a petition," he whispered quietly. He felt them start to take him away. "Be strong, my darling. This will all be over soon, I promise." The strong hands let him away from his beloved Phoebe.

"It won't be okay though, will it?" Stephen said.

"What?"

"You told Phoebe that everything was going to be okay. It won't be, will it?" It was such an innocent comment – the voice of everyone around him.

"Let's see what tomorrow brings, gentlemen."

Brought to the smallest one-room hut he'd ever seen, he was shoved in. There was hardly enough room for him or the four women that stood in it. Elderly, each one studied him with milky eyes. They were blind. He wasn't sure what to do; he couldn't bring himself to attack these women, but he didn't want to passively submit to their sentence, whatever that was.

With surprising speed they were on him, screeching like an unholy terror and pulling at his hair, his clothes, at anything they could find. He was fending off blows as best as he could, but before long they had torn his clothes to shreds. He was shivering as they gathered his clothes in a rough bunch and muttered to themselves: the fabric, the number of tears or holes, the ease with which the cloth tore. He couldn't understand their strange, chittering words. He wouldn't have been surprised if they were speaking another language.

After some time, they seemed to have come to some sort of agreement, because they gathered his clothes and left. How long had passed he didn't know, but soon Stephen and Alfred arrived and held up the leather straps.

"C'mon," they said. With little choice, he held out his wrists as he was shackled. "Look," Alfred said. "I'm really sorry about this, man."

"It's not your fault."

"No, it's yours." Stephen said. "If you'd only have stayed in!"

"It wasn't that simple." The Wanderer said. He turned his attention back to Alfred. "Look after Phoebe if this doesn't end well."

He seemed unable to speak, but simply nodded.

Carrying torches just outside of his hut were all the elders and the old shaman women. Other people peered cautiously around doorways or windows, from around buildings or from other isolated and remote corners. They dragged him outside of the safety of the village and farther still, past the pens used to hold animals and some farmed land. At the boundary of the community was a solid post of wood with notches carved into it for everyone that was sentenced. He was now another notch.

It struck him as they tied him to the post that he didn't remember any of the others. What where their names? How long ago has it been since they were left? Why were they sent out? He realized that the next person tied to this post would probably ponder these same questions and – as he looked at the freshly carved tick in the wood – wouldn't have any idea who he was. After he was tied to the post, the men disappeared behind the shadows of elders and shamans.

The Shamans uttered their strange chirping words while the Elders issued the sentence again; this time loudly enough that the townsfolk – out of sight but well within earshot – would know and understand why this was being done. Then, after a moment of silence, everyone departed.

It was an uncomfortable night. He couldn't sit because of the ties. His shoulders were uncomfortable due to the angle, so he attempted to roll his shoulders as best as he could.

Then the sky started to lighten; it went from the dark inky black of night to a dark blue that promised a new day. He could hear the sounds of the village reinforcing their homes, securing them against the light. His heartbeat faster and an anxious sweat began to bead on his body as his panic began to build. He knew better than to be out right now. It was still safe, but very soon it wouldn't be.

The dark blue continued to lighten and he began to pull uselessly against the leather straps. The sky shifted into lighter and lighter shades and he began to notice shadows forming. The light was nearly there and he was straining as hard as he could to find shelter, but the straps held fast.

Then the horizon erupted and he hated himself for thinking it was beautiful.

Long fingers of light breached the horizon and as he was still in the shadow of the trees, he was able to observe it while in his right mind. It seemed to him odd, he contemplated as he watched the sun come up, that something so deadly, so detrimental, could also be so beautiful. He – like all others – had never seen the sun rise. He'd stopped fighting as he was overwhelmed by the beauty of the day. In the cool of the morning, he had time to reflect on this.

Then the shadows of the trees shrunk as the sun rose higher. Was it minutes or hours? He had no idea as time seemed to suspend. Soon – all too soon – he would be left to the light. He twisted his body as the shadows receded to stay in their protection for as long as he could. What time it was, he didn't know, when the shadows evaded his reach and the light hit him.

His entire body was slammed with warmth, causing chill bumps to rise on his skin. On one hand, it wasn't entirely unpleasant; a gentle, almost maternal embrace that pulled him away from the darkness and into itself. On the other hand, it was utterly terrifying as the sensation of the warmth riddled his entire body.

He wanted to be both of it and free of it. His mind entered into a schizophrenic war with itself, screaming at him to both shun and embrace his newfound self. He squeezed his eyes tightly shut to deny his perception of the light. He screamed at the top of his lungs to drown out the conflicting war within his soul. His muscles tensed and pulled as he sought both to enter the blaze and to hide from it.

Join us, our son.

The strange perceptions started a few hours into his exposure to the light.

Come…

It wasn't a voice in his head, but more like the idea of a voice. He was able to perceive others, their presence, their numbers. The command was so inviting, so welcoming, that he wanted to shred his bonds and run into the new day. He began to pull with renewed vigor, determined this time to break them and run.

But his eyes caught sight of weathered and dead straps; the straps that held other prisoners to this same post, the straps that they in their madness broke and exchanged for life in the Light.

"…no…." he hardly croaked as he his voice was spent from screaming.

Son, do not fight us. We are not your enemy. Join our ranks. Come to us. Come home.

He wanted to. By God did he want it. He squeezed his eyes shut again and pressed his forehead hard into the post; feeling its strength and praying to remain just as anchored.

"No." he said out loud.

Come to us. Come to us. We see your suffering and your pain. We will relieve it. Come.

"NO!"

You will come to us, brother. You always do.

The idea planted in his mind.

But if you do not…

We will come to you.

He was ready to collapse when the townsmen came to get him. It seemed to have taken longer than it should have as people didn't think to check on him. There was a sense of shock among the community. For the first time in living memory, a person left to light did not break free of his bonds and run. He was not consumed by madness.

Only he *was* driven into madness. Faces blended and twisted in his sight; voices echoed or screamed or disappeared. He was looking at the sky one moment and the ground next. Nothing made sense.

They dragged his unusually warm and still glowing body into the village. He was to seek a second judgement. He grunted as he hit the floor. The demon-people of his village continued to taunt him.

"…water…" he croaked.

People avoided him.

"…please…."

He was aware of something wet spilling down most of his arm, but the cup that had been nearly thrown at him was blessedly still somewhat full. He drank it in one shot. It was cool and refreshing and not nearly enough. The room was alive with shouting and raised voices, slamming and thudding. His head reverberated with the noise.

He could hardly move. His body screamed in protest. He simply allowed himself to lay still, face planted against the cool earth. He felt it then; an almost outside command. His legs were twitching as if trying to obey a direction to rise. His hands were clenching as if commanded to throttle. His shoulders burned in tension.

He was too tired, that no matter what the Light tried to convince his worn body to do, it could not obey it.

He heard a loud thud and then blissful silence.

"You have not been driven mad," a voice said. He kept his eyes closed.

"No."

"You returned to us."

"Yes."

"Look at me."

"I can't."

"Have you been blinded?" He chuckled sardonically.

"I've been left exhausted, sir."

"You are not of us anymore, but of the Light; yet you do not behave as someone of the Light," the elder mused.

He had no idea which elder it was.

"So I will allow you to remain here."

He felt relief wash over him, even to drown out the outrage of the others.

"You will go out during the day, as the light will no longer harm you and ensure our cattle are protected from the wolves and other beasts. Guard them to ensure we have food, and you will earn your place."

He was lifted bodily off the ground and thrown into the same small hut that they had stripped him in. He grunted as he hit the ground. The three shamans were there. They continued to study him with their milky eyes, but right now he didn't care.

"Where's….Phoebe?" he asked.

"Hush, boy," one of the women said.

He resented being called a boy, but the woman was old enough that she could call half the elders 'boy' and get away with it. They wrapped him considerably more gently into clothes than the force they used to pull them off of him. He could hear sloshing and something moving and realized that they were providing a meal for him.

"Where's Phoebe?" he asked again.

"At home, where she belongs."

"I want to see her," he said.

He once again felt his body trying to lunge, to attack, to maim. He seemed to be regaining some strength back as it took a more concentrated effort to prevent himself from doing so.

"She's been told where you are. She will come if she wishes. You, however, will stay here."

The woman that spoke stared in his direction defiantly, as if to daring him to challenge her.

He didn't. He was already on the knife's edge and one misstep would lead to the end of his allowance in the community.

He was able to sit up and was handed a bowl. He drank greedily, his body being reminded of how long he'd been shackled, how thirsty he was. The bowl was snatched from him quickly, hardly letting him finish it before it was again pressed in his hands. This pattern repeated until he had his fill and shoved the bowl away.

She didn't come, he thought as he lay down. *She's not here.* Food was given, but the ache in his chest turned his stomach from such things. Instead, he lay curled up and before he even realized what happened, he had drifted to sleep.

He awoke suddenly, the slamming of windows alerting him to the day. The heavy curtain flapped uselessly against the wind and in a panic he was driven away from the light with a hiss. He stood, clutching the wall like a fool until somewhere in the recesses of his mind he heard a faint drumbeat: it was his heart, spelling out the horrors of the day before. His job was now to ensure safety for the cattle. With a sigh, he dragged his shoes on and mentally prepared himself to step into that brutal light.

The food they had offered him yesterday (now hardened bread and a bruised apple), sat outside the door. He shook off the ants that had begun their feast and stuffed it in his mouth. He had no telling the next time he'd eat.

The thing that he noticed first was again the warmth. He stood for a few minutes to savor it. It took a moment to realize he was walking into the village. He had a rusty hatchet and he stepped into the shadows to begin breaking down one of the wooden shutters.

It was the startled scream from inside as he hit it once that pierced through the command to destroy. He willed himself to drop the hatchet, but he didn't have that much control. His arm raised as is if on its own accord and at the last second he opened his hand and the hatchet slipped through his fingers. His shoulder smarted as his hand slammed into the shutters. He was panting heavily.

He went back to his small hut and found a shirt with longer sleeves. He covered as much as he could- he did not want to be left to the mercy of the light.

He had some experience with cattle in the past, though the animals looked at him with no small amount of surprise that he was out in broad daylight. He rubbed the nose of one of the oxen affectionately; he snorted and went back to grazing contentedly. He found a blackthorn branch that he manipulated into a considerable weapon.

He secured the perimeter of the fence and repaired some damage that was difficult to see in the dark, but he now realized it was more damaged than assessed. He was learning how to feel the force of the light's control, and how to combat it.

Why will you not join us? The ideas in his head swirled. *You know you do not want this needless suffering.*

"Leave me alone," he growled. The horse in front of him looked up curiously. Perhaps he was driven mad by the light after all. "I have made my choice and will enjoy my days in peace."

They'll throw you out and you know it. The idea was hard on him now. Angry. *It's only a matter of time before the ones that squeal and scream like rats will be driven out of their holes.*

"Leave me be!"

He swung his walking stick with greater force than he meant at weeds. He had struck a horse's foot, who loudly protested, rearing up on his legs and kicking. He had to duck to avoid the well-deserved lashing.

The rest of the day he spent in silence, though he felt like he was being watched. He was constantly looking at the shadows of the trees just past the Shadowless Post as he worked, expecting more of the people of the Light to come out. No one did, but he could sense their presence in the same way that a lover knew upon waking that they were alone: Instead of an emptiness and sense of vacancy about him, there was a presence and a sense of arrival. The voices had threatened to come. He bandaged the horse's leg, and the animal was forgiving. He glanced back toward the trees.

They were coming.

That night he went to his newly assigned home and was surprised to see Phoebe there. She looked ashen and unwell and the moment he saw her all his bitter thoughts of her abandonment dispelled with an overwhelming desire.

"Phoebe!"

He ran to her in several strides, despite the protestations of his body and pulled her into a tight embrace. The smell of her hair-always earthy and sweet – filled his lungs and was the nectar his body needed. She was stiff, he realized, and afraid, but after a moment she clutched him as if he was a raft in the tumultuous sea of their situation.

"I've been so worried," she sobbed.

"I'm alright." He rocked her and hugged her. "Why didn't you come yesterday?"

Her spirit broke then and she shuddered as she buried her face deeply in her hands and cried.

"I was afraid," he made out through her sobs. "I didn't know what had happened to you! They said at first that you were burnt and red like a cake, then they said you were well, then they said you'd become some kind of monster, I –"

He didn't let her finish but held her.

"It's over. It told you it would be."

"But you're one of them now," she said. The fear in her eyes tore through him. "I don't know how I can trust you anymore."

"Phoebe, my darling," he said, again pulling her into his embrace. "I'm still me. It's still the man you married."

She framed his face with shaking hands, searching his eyes and face deeply for evidence. He seemed to have passed this inspection, because she threw her arms around his neck and held him so tightly he thought she would break.

"I miss you," she said.

"I'm right here, my love."

But she sat away from him and shook her head.

"No – you're not." Choking, she left him alone to stare after her.

He had something like a fever dream. He was standing alone in a dead forest; the trees around him were burnt and in some places still glowing in embers, their dead branches shaking fists at the sky in rage. The smoke from this assault had long ago vanished, leaving a once well-trodden path blanketed in ash. The rocks bore the scars of their tree brethren, though one could feel the heat of this day remembered on their surfaces.

A sense of great sadness filled this place; and a sense of dread. He could feel wicked delight everywhere around him: a celebration at the downfall of this once lush place. He alone mourned. As he continued to walk the path, choking back his emotion, the trees began to change.

At first one appeared to be a horse; the branches twining to as it pawed at the air, its mouth open in a silent scream. He had started at the sight, thinking it a real animal until he saw the flakes of leaves and bark. An odd illusion then.

The next appeared a bull, and so to with a ram and, one tree brought low, crouching like a wolf on the hunt. He paused a hand on the trunk of the horse, remembering with clarity the way he had struck it.

"I'm sorry, my friend." He said to the burned thing. "I never met to harm you."

But the horse's mane, now devoid of its lush green foliage, hardly stirred. He continued on.

Soon the trees began to appear human-like: dryads left in frozen agony. They appeared in numerous forms and stretched as far as he could see. Some were reaching to the heavens as if in plea. Some were hunched, as if attempting to uproot themselves and so escape. Others embraced their burning as if somehow deserving of such horrid retribution. Some were cradling infants and small children, others searched frantically for loved ones in the ensuing chaos.

"Phoebe," he hardly whispered.

For some reason, the dream brought to mind his wife and he sought fruitlessly among the ashen faces for that of his beloved.

38

Thorns and thistles grasped him and he beat them away with vigor and enthusiasm, letting nothing stop his frantic search.

He broke through to a somewhat barren glade, housing only one single large oak tree in its center. This tree, though singed, appeared unharmed. The sight of something salvaged, something *saved* from such destruction made his heart swell. He took one step toward the oak's majesty –

His face was pressed deeply into the earth and many grasping thorns wound around him, pinning him down.

No, not thorns. Hands.

It took several minutes to realize he was in the village – a side street by the bakers if he wasn't mistaken – and was being forcibly pinned to the ground. He grunted as he tried to dispel the strange dream and orient himself. How did he get outside? When did he get outside? What times was it? What happened? Where was Phoebe?

These questions cycled through his mind with no answer forthcoming.

"Get back into your hut, son of Light," one of the men growled as they dragged him back, feet against the rocks and packed earth.

"I never left," he protested gently. "Why was I taken out?"

"You left, alright. Killed Sam and ran through the town attacking anyone who came near you." The voice was flat, nearly dead. It was a combination of the voice and the words that chilled him.

"Wait, what? What happened?"

He needn't have asked however, as he saw them dragging a body away as they approached the hut. Thomas – a man considerably bigger and more threatening – was taking his place. The look he shot him was of pure hatred. They threw him in and slammed the door shut behind them.

"WAIT! What happened?"

But only silence greeted him. He beat uselessly against the door for a few moments before he sat back down on the bed and stared at his hands. They were dirty and streaked with what appeared to be blood. He rubbed them vigorously but the red would not come off. He sighed as his head thudded against the wall.

So the light could control his body when he wasn't in his waking moments. He wanted to allow himself to weep, but his body would not find tears. Instead he closed his eyes and chastised the laughter in his head before going back to sleep.

He heard the sound of the town preparing for day, so he roused himself. This time no food was left, and he didn't think he'd be able to stomach it if it was. He ignored the animals and walked until he reached the forest. Pausing only briefly for a moment, he pushed his way into the underbrush. Once in deeply enough he felt secure in the shadows, he began to work.

Weeks passed like this. He would go missing for sometimes days or weeks at a time. He always came back and sent word to Phoebe to see him and she would always come. She would ask where he had been? What took so long? He was supposed to look after the animals! Every time he left, she believed him succumbed to the madness and run away forever. What was he playing at?

The dream was the same every night, yet he was always denied the right to see the tree. He wanted so badly that he would awaken with a pain in his chest.

Sometimes, as he was gone on his errands, he would awaken to find himself having traveled in his sleep *back*. He didn't yet want to go back, so he set about rope and tied himself in place.

The voices were more persistent, laughing at his attempts at a normal life, always whispering how close they were. He threatened them, warned them, and spent time every night telling

Thomas to warn the others: People of the Light were coming. His cries always fell on deaf ears.

That night was a quiet night. He summoned for Phoebe and Bethany to arrive, to do so with haste and dressed in clothes for traveling. The request was peculiar at best and he paced his small hut as he waited. Would she come? Would she do ask he asked? Finally she arrived and he pulled her into his arms tightly.

"Bless God you've come!" He said, holding her at arm's length.

"What is going on?" She demanded. "You asked such strangeness, I had a mind not to listen."

"I'm glad you did. It's time for me to tell you what I've been doing." He ran to the bed and pulled out a rough map. "I've been warning everyone that the Light is coming but they won't listen, so I've made an escape for you and Bethany."

She blanched, but did not interrupt him.

"Every shelter is one night's walk apart. Go to one and rest until its dark. Then the next. The last one will give you one night's walk from the next village. They will take you in and you'll be safe there. This place will not stand much longer."

"We must tell them," She said, making for the door.

"I've *been* telling them!" He said. "They will not listen. So I've made a way for you to be safe. Please…"

She studied him carefully, then took the map.

"When should I leave?"

"At once. I'm surprised they haven't come yet. I've been trying to dissuade them or throw them off course but they are nearly here. It won't be but a day or two more and I want you gone."

She nodded.

"I'll not see you again, will I?"

"When you get the village, find yourself happiness. I will have you in my heart always. Now go."

She took two steps to the door before turning back and kissing him with the same passion she once did. In that moment everything that had happened hadn't and they were once again young, in love, and brave. The spell she cast was broken as quickly as her movement and she left.

He heard it first. He had hardly time to reflect on what he had just done then he heard her scream. He knew her voice instantly and ran to the door, beating it. But his cries were unheard in the roar of chaos. Flames flickered and burned and men and women screamed as they were cut down in the street.

"Phoebe! NO! Let me out!"

Suddenly the door opened and he was horrified to see other people of the Light looking back at him. He recognized them instantly the way one would recognize a friend, even after many years. A sensation of a deviled kinship.

"We told you we were coming," the one who opened the door for him said. "Thank you for leading us right to them."

With an animalistic cry, he threw himself at the gloating man. They went down into a tumble of limbs.

He hit him again and again, bloodying his hands in the violence. He was hauled off of the spitting child of Light by others and thrown into the ground. The hard earth cleared his vision of the rage that had driven him and he became aware of heat and flames, the stench of blood and bodies, and the twisted smell of death. He let out a startled gasp as he was looking into the now lifeless eyes of Phoebe. Bethany was a little way away, unmoving.

"No...." he could hardly breathe the word. He crawled to her body, cradling it as his entire world went up in smoke.

He traveled by day and slept by night. During the day the laughing tangled mess of voices in his head goaded him out, encouraging him to find some place to rest. He knew they were watching him, knew they were studying his every movement.

He didn't care.

After the village was destroyed, he'd been beaten by the attackers and left for dead. He had stayed in that spot, broken and useless for days, lost in his misery and grief.

After four days he finally roused himself. He went into the remains of a shack and found food. He scarfed it down but took no joy in the eating. He quenched himself with cool, clear water that he hadn't tasted in ages.

He went to the Shadowless Post, and there he dug. How many days or nights he dug he had no idea, but he dug until his hands bled, until he could taste the salt of his sweat.

Leave them... the voices in his head demanded. *They are rats, hiding from the light in dark shadows. They are vermin. Leave them exposed to the glorious day in death that they did not embrace in life.*

He ignored their demands. He dug.

It was just past dusk when he lowered the bodies of his wife and daughter into the grave he built. He took care to bury some of his friends and family as well; taking them from this despicable light into the resting place of eternal darkness. Those that condemned him, those that he hated in life...

He buried them also.

He stuck a wreath of flowers on the post, and he lit a torch that he staked into the ground. He wasn't going to blow it out; he would let it burn until there was nothing left and the graves were baptized by ashes.

He found the healthiest prize bull of their flock and tethered it. The rest of the animals he opened the gate and let them loose. Perhaps they would find new homes. Perhaps they wouldn't. It didn't matter to him now.

He followed the path he had originally cut for his wife and after a week and a half, made it to the next village. He was received suspiciously, but he gave the prized bull as an offering to the community. He explained that he could work during the daytime hours. He explained that his village had been ravaged.

They took him in and he was put to work.

A month later they came.

He escaped again and they let him go. So it continued. He would wander until he found a village, they would take him in and the children of the light would come. After five villages he'd taken to living in the forest. He didn't want the deaths of anymore on his head. The voices in his head called to him, summoned him.

He ran away from them.

He came across a settlement that appeared abandoned. It didn't have the burnt, acrid scent of the destroyed. Just…empty.

He found new clothes and burned the old blood and dirt stained ones. He kept his body entirely covered. He found a deep hooded cowl to wear. He sat on the ground, watching the sun set. He couldn't bring himself to weep as the last rays went down. Once it was dark, he took a knife. He wanted to blind himself there in that village. He didn't want to see the light nor did he want the light to see him. He tested the sharpness of the blade. It was dull and rusted. It would probably infect him. Kill him.

He pressed against his eye and began to push. He felt the pressure first, followed by the pain. In one quick, violent twist, he pulled his eye out. He felt warm blood running down his face and he pressed his hand to his eye. He cried out in agony, but the physical pain was only one small token of his suffering.

He threw his head back, the hot rivulets of blood running down his cheek and let his torment, his loss, his uncertainty rock the sky.

What are you doing? The voices hissed. *Stop this madness! This darkness has reached your soul deeply. Come to the light, our son. Child, stop!*

As he reached for the knife with a shaking hand, he felt something and reached for it. It was a pair of goggles. They were a little scratched but dark tinted. He stuffed some padding into the now empty socket and pressed the goggles on his face. Perhaps he would finish the job another day. Exhausted and hurting, he lay down and slept.

He continued on. It was another day. He stopped to clean his wound by a stream and drink to refresh his soul. He then put the goggles back on.

Where are you…? The voices wondered. *My child, come back to us.*

"Shut up," he said to the voice.

It was the day after he realized that the light could not see through the darkness. By wearing his goggles, he prevented them from know his location. By covering his skin, the rays of their reach couldn't find him. He was now, truly, alone.

And for the first time since he sentenced that boy to die, the Wanderer laughed.

The elder board was silent, and he could nearly hear the sound of the people outside, crowding the entrance and listening.

"How many villages have been lost?" one of the elders asked.

"In total? I have no idea. But many more have been saved by having me around. I ask only for a respite from my travels. I do not stay longer than one year in any one place. In such a time, I will serve you during the day; protecting your animals from harm as well as look for any warning signs and weaknesses that are easier to see in the daylight than are visible at night. That is if you'll have me."

Explosive argument followed. There was mad gesturing and adamant shouting. The Wanderer waited in silence.

"ENOUGH!" the head Elder screamed. He slammed his staff down and after a moment the others went silent. "I've heard both the request and its opposition. There is much to say for both. However, I also realize our people have needs that are my primary

45

concern and a man who addresses himself only as Wanderer is of little concern to me."

Everyone waited.

"Some of our livestock have been going missing in the daylight hours and we don't know what is causing it. It seems a sentinel for a brief time may help root the problem and give us a chance to determine the next course of action and secure food for our people. You are to stay here by the terms you set into place: no more than one year. Distract and deter the sons of Light from coming here and you will earn our gratitude and perhaps another welcome. Agreed?"

"Agreed."

"Good. Then Ilya will show you to your hut. You mentioned wounds that need addressing?"

"Yes sir."

"I'll send the grandmother to see to it. Now out."

The Wanderer followed the young man, who was clearly displeased, in silence. He had learned over his various times as "guest" the less he said the better. He wanted to be as invisible as possible. The hut was every bit as he remembered every other hut to be: small and neglected; often the holding place of criminals and the dangerous. It was, oddly enough, home to him. He'd been in nothing but these prisons for so long he had hard time imagining life outside of them.

He found a chamber pot, as well as a wash basin and a pitcher of water. The thing that caught his attention the most, however, was the steaming tub. It seems that while the council was deciding his fate someone had anticipated the chance that he would be welcomed in and tried to make the cell as homey as possible.

After using the chamber pot, he took all the lampshades off the candles to allow himself enough light to see. He stripped down gladly and slid into the blessedly warm water. He hadn't had a bath in months and a hot bath in years. His body tensed all at once and the cramp had him hissing out his breath; the steam fogged his goggles. A moment more and his muscles started to relax. He stayed in the water until it was starting to get cold, then he washed himself quickly and stepped out. He heard a brisk knock on the door and knowing that the grandmother was always blind bid whoever it was to enter without much thought. Nimue came in and set a tray down. He hastily tried to cover himself and she chuckled softly under her breath.

"Don't cover yourself on my account. I've seen a man before."

"I don't...I didn't mean," he said, still holding the thin blanket from the bed around his waist. She laughed now, which embarrassed him. "What?"

"I never imagined someone who can stand up to the light being shy."

"I'm not shy, but someone coming in like this will make anyone startle."

She shrugged as she began to dish his meal for him. "I suppose that's true."

"You're young for a grandmother," he said a bit gruffly, trying to hide his earlier mistake.

"I'm not a grandmother; she's attending to other matters so I offered to come in her stead. She still will see you, but clean you up I suppose anyone can do." She wrung a cloth in a bowl. "I'd need you to undress anyway, so I can see what's hurting you."

"Nothing and everything."

"I'm sure of it. Why don't you lie down on the bed and I'll see what shall be seen."

He did as directed. He felt the light attempt to control his body; his arms, legs, and anything else, but in the last near decade he'd learn how to control the impulses. She carefully examined him, cleaning him here or there. He winced reflexively when she hit a tender spot on his back. She heard her sudden intake of breath and the momentary hesitation of alarm.

"What?"

"This is a very nasty wound; it looks like it may have the wound disease. I'll need help." she said, immediately getting to her feet. "This must have been brutal."

"I don't remember it," he said, trying to see the spot that caused concern. "I do believe that the light has changed how I can understand pain; perhaps to keep me moving when my body really wants rest."

"Or maybe you're just human and tired. Give me a minute and I'll go get grandmother."

He wanted so badly to ask that she not leave him but he knew it was foolishness to do so. He was enveloped in a cold loneliness. He tried to reach this spot or see it but to no avail. Instead, he spent more productive time trying to remember any injury to him that perhaps he had forgotten.

The door opened and he looked to see Nimue return with an old woman. Unlike most grandmothers, she was not blind. She held her hands up as if she was placating a wild animal.

"I understand there's a terrible hurt. Please," she said, offering her hands to him. "Allow me."

"Of course, Grandmother," he said, turning to face the wall again.

She gently prodded and poked and could feel wet run down his back. She muttered to herself. Whatever was back there stung and burned; sometimes at once. Finally she sat back.

"It's not as bad as I've seen in the past, but it's still a nasty wound. Do you recall how you've gotten it?"

He shook his head. "No, grandmother."

"I'll have to open the wound; it seems to have begun to heal, but something is trapped in there that is making it fever and

48

cry." She turned to Nimue. "I need a pair of tongs and three knives of increasing size, a large needle, and some good dried sheep gut."

"Yes grandmother."

He had an idea what all of this was for, but didn't want to ask and confirm it. He kept his face to the wall while she poked and prodded his back. He didn't move as she felt skin, scabs, and who knew what else. She gently mopped him up as she worked. His back was first wet, then only cold as the air struck it.

Nimue came in and he could hear the metallic clinking as she provided the tools. There was a sharp pain as the grandmother began scrapping one of the blades along his back.

More blood.

It was much to his surprise that Nimue came to the other side and caressed his face gently, taking his hand.

"There's a sizable something in there; she'll get it out. Grandmother has such deft hands," she said with a small smile by way of encouragement.

He didn't want to risk choking out some word after his earlier embarrassment, so he nodded. His back felt on fire, and yet the grandmother hummed as she worked as if she was embroidering a pillow.

He could feel the strange sensation of her digging *in* his back. A sharp pinch as she hit something and he involuntarily jumped. Grandmother jumped.

"STAY STILL!" she hissed at him and then went back to digging.

There was an agonizingly slow process of him feeling something moving around in his flesh as she moved delicately. Then a sudden release and a slight ooze of blood. Grandmother cackled.

"Ah –ha! There you are!" Wanderer heard a clanging sound as she dropped whatever it was into a dish.

49

"Nimue, come here and make this poultice for me," grandmother instructed.

"Of course."

She squeezed his hand and it was as much to his surprise as anything that he held tightly for a minute more. It'd been so long that he had gentle human contact he didn't want to lose it. She offered him a smile and slipped out of his grip, coming to help grandmother.

His back was cleaned and stitched. Finally, some sort of grainy poultice was applied and the entire thing was wrapped.

"Finish cleaning him up, child," Grandmother said, struggling to get up. "I've got to get back to the elders."

"Of course." There was silence for a few minutes as Nimue continued to bandage him.

"What was in me?" the Wanderer asked.

"Bit of metal of some kind."

She showed him the dish. It was an oblong rusted piece that was difficult to determine. He had no idea where it came from, but was grateful they found it and removed it.
"You should rest now. You'll have a busy day tomorrow."

He wanted to ask Nimue not to leave, but before he could, she was gone.

The days blended. His wound went from a constant throb to an occasional sharp reminder, to a scar. He worked all day, supervising the animals, helping to build fencing and enclosures seeing things in the light that were easy to miss in the dark. He was able to find edible berries and plants that in the dark could be mistaken for more deadly cousins and increase his own food stores.

The animals, he realized, were not being taken by wolves or bears: instead, a weakness in the fence allowed for some to slip either over or under. He repaired it.

50

Like all places, he wasn't always remembered during feedings.

At night, he would watch the children. It was a strange change to his expected routine. At first it was Nimue bringing her son for him to bond with. She would use the time he was away to do medicines for the people that the grandmothers were too busy or too ignorant to care for. She was well on her way to becoming a grandmother herself one day.

Wanderer appreciated the company.

Then, little by little, a few other mothers would ask him to watch their children while they tended to this task or that. He thought to refuse them, but soon his hut became a hotbed of childish delight and it refreshed his soul in a way that little else would be able to.

It took about two months at his best guess until the wound was mostly healed. After that he was working so hard during the day he was often too exhausted to watch the children at night. He still opened his doors once a week – on Thursdays – to them to come, but the rest of the time he needed rest.

Nimue visited him every day. She insisted that he did not miss a single meal though she had no reason to care or obligation to do so.

"Won't your husband mind?" he asked her one such visit. He didn't need the ire of a jealous mate to challenge his already precarious standing.

"I don't have one," she said simply, though finally. It was a sensitive subject and asked no more.

This town was different from all the others. For the first time since he was cursed by the light, he felt like he belonged.

The children visiting him, the companionship from Nimue, the fact that he was not neglected. He felt like he was finally home after so much searching. He was careful to enjoy every moment of it while not becoming too attached; he would have to leave this place, just like he left all the others. That sensation alone filled him with a sense of melancholy, as it was the first time he didn't want to leave.

He began to feel the presence of the light around seven months. He was constantly watching out for them, being extra diligent to make sure he had no contact with them. His goggles were cleaned by Nimue every night while he had his eye closed to ensure that he could clearly see. His cowl was deep, his gloves free of holes. It was not unprecedented. The Light would make rounds on their own. Several town visits he made had such encounters where the light would move right along, oblivious to his presence.

Perhaps it was attachment to this place. Perhaps it was an innate sense of something being wrong. Whatever it was, he didn't like it.

When Nimue came to his room that evening, he noticed her son was not with her.

"Where's the boy?" Wanderer asked as he gratefully accepted the bowl she handed him. She closed the door behind her.

"He's with the other children today." She said as she sat down.

"Ah. I miss seeing that little guy." Nimue smiled.

"He's taken quite a liking to you." They ate in silence for a few minutes.

"Something is on your mind?"

She shook her head.

"You may tell me if you like."

"Do you really have to go?" she blurted out. Her face flushed and she looked a little embarrassed.

"I promised the elders that within a year I would be gone. Unless they ask me to stay, I must leave."

"Maybe we can petition them," she said.

Wanderer shook his head.

"It's unlikely. There will be very little reason for them to keep me here."

"What do you mean with such talk?" she said with surprising force. He was taken away by it. "You've saved our livestock more than once! You fixed our fencing and secured our protective walls! You've increased our food stores and stabilized buildings, not to mention provided a welcome relief to stressed-out mothers."

"I don't mind the work, but if I stay past my allotted time, it'll be worse for us."

She cocked an eyebrow. "Us?"

"Yes." The Wanderer said unapologetically. "I'll be kicked out for certain, if not killed. If you think they do not realize the time you're spending with me then you are mistaken. I fear for you as well."

"You needn't." She finished eating and set her bowl aside. "I wanted to ask you something."

"You are welcome to." She slid closer to him.

"Would you take me?"

"What?" He recoiled but she was fast and grabbed his arm.

"I'm a woman who takes the things I want," she said directly. "And I have been spending time trying to decide how I felt about you. You saved my son when you had no obligation to. For that I was thankful. You have then protected my community, for which I am grateful. But you've also defended me when no one else in this community will and for that I am stunned. I'm an outcast here," she said to his bewildered look.

"But aren't you the next grandmother?" He sputtered.

"Perhaps – but not if the current three have their way. I eat with you because there is none here that will allow me to join them. I see in you a kindred broken spirit; and more than that, a man. It is the man that I have come to love and respect. I would go with you if I could face the light, but I cannot. You will not stay and I understand your reason, or I would ask to wed you. Since I cannot go with you and you cannot stay, I ask that we take this moment and pretend."

"Nimue…."

"I know what I'm asking." she said. He cradled her face in his rough, calloused hands. "I do not want you to think I'm easy or simply had. I'm not. However, I would be yours for a short time, that I should taste acceptance." Her eyes searched his face diligently.

"You are a fine woman. Any man would surely want you for his own."

"I care not for any man. Just you."

A thousand warring thoughts raced through the Wanderer's mind; all the reasons he should and all the reasons he shouldn't. She disrobed before him and he still had time to shun her away.

"Take off your goggles," she said.

He shook his head.

"I dare not."

"I want you to see me undistorted and I want to see your eyes."

He hesitated.

"Please."

He was inside anywhere and there were no landmarks, no clues as to where he was. He searched inside to find the presence of the light, looking for evidence of them probing him for location. He found none. Before he could second guess himself, he took the goggles off. He turned his head away, ashamed of the socket where his eye had once been.

She came to him and straddled his lap. She caressed his face as planted a kiss gently on his forehead.

"It's beautiful." she whispered.

He closed his eyes, breathed in her scent and kissed her.

He was out in the field when he heard it: the screaming. Dropping the logs he was using to reinforce a fence, he ran straight for the village. He tore his goggles off as they were useless now.

It was engulfed. People of the light were breaking down doors and killing everyone inside.

Rage boiled in him only matched by the destruction of his village. This time, however, he was prepared. He pulled knives out of his boots that he forged in darkness; twisted metal of rage and vengeance that fit comfortably in his hands. He cut down three people on his way to Nimue's house, hardly aware of his actions. For the first time since his curse, he allowed the light to give him control.

But he used it against them. The light added strength to his muscles, endurance to his limbs. Instead of finding those in the huts, he used that momentum against the light walkers, having no time for either pity or remorse.

Nimue's door held, but it was facing quite the assault. He recognized the man in the front. He was no longer a boy now and his frame had filled in. With a cry, the Wanderer threw himself again at the boy.

The boy went down with a grunt and lay stunned. For a moment his eyes registered shock and fear as if the light temporarily let him go. But it was over as quickly as it started and his eyes became that of a killer.

"There you are, our son," Wanderer heard in his mind.

The boy's eyes became blank and seemed to glow- the pulsing lights that affected those that were touched by the light seemed to race. Others in the area turned as if picking up on his signal. The Wanderer also understood the message- the Children of the Light were being directed at him; but he, being one of them was not identified as threat. They continued on their mission.

The Wanderer didn't waste time on platitudes; he sunk his fist into the boy's face. The first time sent a shock up his hand. The second he felt the satisfaction of one of his teeth coming out, and the third missed, given there was so much blood that his hand slipped. The boy managed to throw him off and spit out blood and what remained of his teeth. The Wanderer twirled his knives to ensure a firm grip.

"I've not much of a taste for blood, but I am really going to enjoy killing you." The boy smiled.

"You're the treasonous son. You are the wolf in sheep's clothing who is a son of light who lives in darkness."

The Wanderer didn't bite, but instead lunged. The boy turned quickly and evaded the point of the blade. Before the Wanderer could turn he felt a crack on the back of his head. He was momentarily stunned.

"Why do you fight us? Join us," the voice of the light said.

"I haven't started fighting yet," Wanderer growled.

His vision still blurred. He righted himself in time to avoid another blow of the rock that the boy had picked up. They circled each other like cats, carefully measuring steps. The echoing cry of torment screamed around them but he was unable to take his eyes off the man responsible for the suffering and death of his family.

The boy eventually dropped the rock and held his arms out, a father preparing to embrace a child.

"Join us!"

The pull to join the light was greater in that moment than at any other time. Wanderer almost collapsed. A sound reached him and he saw Nimue's door finally give. He knew what horror awaited her. It steeled his resolve.

The Wanderer screamed and ran at the boy, who was able to avoid every swing of the blades. He danced lightly on his feet, a pirouette and ended up behind the Wanderer. He spun to meet his opponent, but the knife sliced only through air.

Again and again he slashed with his knife, and again and again he missed. It seemed that while Wanderer had spent the last seven years searching for a home, the boy spent the last seven years learning how to kill.

The Wanderer lurched forward as he was thrust from behind. He used his momentum to spin, landing on his back instead of his stomach- and in the process avoided a pitchfork that quivered as it stuck in the ground. With a startled gasp at the sight, the boy stepped on his wrist, causing the Wanderer to scream in pain.

The boy ground his foot deeper into the hand, and as the Wanderer screamed he reached into his boot and grabbed his other knife, driving it deeply into the boy's thigh. The boy roared and collapsed off of him. The Wanderer's hand was swelling and virtually useless, but he still had his left, and he brandished his knife feebly.

"We will not forget!"

The boy spat more blood as he grimaced and yanked the knife out of his thigh. The first sound he made was almost a whimper when the angry blank eyes graced his features again.

"These rats will die! Their whole sniveling existence will be exterminated!"

"They will not!" Wanderer snapped back.

The boy smiled then, a demonic heartless grin as he sent a signal to all those around. Suddenly the senses around Wanderer were amplified: the screams as people were cut down, the smell of burning bodies, and anguished moaning as the children of the light disgraced the last of the survivors.

The Wanderer forced control of his senses as he sized up the boy. His strength and energy were waning and his heart broke at the devastating loss around him. He screamed as the boy threw the knife and while it was not a deep wound it sliced his arm deeply. He collapsed, bleeding and exhausted.

"Why, you fool?" he finally spat. "Why do you let the light control you? Why do you not fight it?"

The boy, now weaponless, picked up a rock.

"*We are one- there is no you, me, or I. Except you. We will not forget.*" He contemplated the stone. "*Primal, common. It seems fitting to kill you this way.*"

The boy charged and it was with a surge of satisfaction that the Wanderer felt his last knife slide into the boy's ribs like butter. He gave a gargled, choking sound and looked down wide-eyed and surprised. The Wanderer attempted to finish the boy with a quick twist, but it seemed that the boy was determined to win. He hefted the rock high above his head and as Wanderer grabbed for the handle of the knife and started to twist, his world went black.

He awoke and it was earlier in the day than he remembered. There was a sickly scent of smoke still in the air, mingled with the scent of blood and death. It was something he knew.

"Nimue?" He croaked, trying to get up. "NIMUE!"

He dragged himself despite the sticky mess that was the back of his crushed skull. There were large dark spots of blood on the ground, but the boy was gone. If he survived, or if he would survive, the Wanderer did not know or care.

Nimue was, like all the others, like Phoebe all those years ago, left dead. He cradled her lifeless form and wept. As soon as he could stand, he tended to his wounds. He ignored the pain as he stitched himself and wrapped his hand as tightly as he could.

He went to work, digging. It was just after dusk when he lowered the bodies the grave. Just like before, he buried those that were kind to him: the mothers and children that showed him welcome. Those that condemned him, those that he hated in life…

He buried them also.

He rested in the ruins that day and cleaned himself with water of the blood and vileness that covered him.

He slept without dreams. In his sleep, the light raged at his betrayal. He promised to learn the skill of the blade. He would not run, but he would hunt. The light mocked him. He awoke and it was the next day or the day after- he didn't know. He couldn't yet move.

The next night he dreamt of the same, this time he got to the tree. Its shade was cool and sweet and in it he saw his promise etched into its bark. He awoke with new purpose. He covered himself completely and packed whatever food he could carry.

It was with the same grief that he left his hometown that he prepared to leave this one. It was as he was leaving that he heard a soft coo.

His eyes widened and he tore into the house, upending everything. Safely hidden from the light under a basket and wrapped in a blanket was Nimue's son. His face broke into an excited grin when he saw the Wanderer and he reached for him. How he'd remained silent this whole time, the Wanderer didn't know. He may not have had to; in the confusion and the noise, it wasn't unlikely that a child crying could have gotten lost.

"My strong boy," he said, pulling the child into his arms.

The baby wiggled slightly, but soon settled into the bigger man's embrace. The Wanderer held him in front of him.

"I'm sorry I never learned your name but if you allow me I will grant you one of my own. I will call you Phoebus, after my wife. Your mother loved you very much. If you allow me to be your father, I will care for you in a dark world. I am of the light, boy, but you will be the light of my life."

The baby giggled and stuffed his fist in his mouth.

It was still dark after he fed the boy, and the Wanderer knew that he could make it to a good hiding place well before dawn. With the baby tied to his back, the Wanderer left in search of rest.

Nearing the dawn, the Wanderer found a suitable place. Unknown to him, a brief ray of light touched the child. Phoebus was attracted to the glittering light. The light, giddy, reached for the child- but could not claim him- for that child was loved by both light and darkness. Wanderer placed him deep in the den he had made.

That child was hope. That child was Shadow.

COCK AND CHICK

By Lindsay Lake

Baby Cock Rooster, his brothers, and cousins fought in the farmyard, in a playful way, of course, like baby roosters do.

One day they played in the henhouse when the hens feasted in the yard, picking at the bugs and seeds on the ground. They happened to knock over a nest and the eggs went flying, rolling all over the ground. The baby roosters knocked the eggs around like they were playing ice hockey, kicking them, and bouncing them off the chicken coop walls. One cracked. Cock Rooster spied the crack and blocked the others from kicking it. The cousins teased him and fought him. Cock really didn't know what the egg involved, but he guarded the egg so fiercely his brothers called him names. Eventually they laughed at him, gave up, and walked away.

Alone in the henhouse, Cock looked out the door at his brothers and cousins playing in the yard. He didn't know what alone was. He had never been alone before. Not for one second since his birth. Not only had he never been alone he'd never disagreed with his brothers and cousins before. He felt fear and excitement at the same time.

He heard a popping noise. The egg cracked further. Cock Rooster watched in amazement. He watched a long time. He watched as the fluffy yellow chick struggled her way out of the shell. Chick was born. She lived. She was alive. Her feathers the color of the sun. Cock had never seen anything so cute and fuzzy. They stared into each other's eyes for what seemed like eternity.

The farm dog, smelling fresh birth, pushed his way into the chicken coop. Cock's feathers stood on end. He danced around like a loony bird and crowed louder than he had ever crowed in his life. The farm dog, thinking Cock had cracked up, backed off.

"What's one cracked egg anyway," the farm dog said in his stupid flat voice. "There will be more before the day is through."

Cock Rooster surprised himself and shocked himself that he could be so angry. He managed to help Chick get back in her nest. He let the dog take care of the afterbirth shell.

Cock didn't go far from the coop after that. Even when his baby rooster cousins teased him and called him "chick-whipped." Oh ... he'd fight with them and play rough with them but he always had one eye on Chick's nest. He talked to her every time her mother went out into the yard to eat.

It didn't take long… just a blink of a Rooster's eye before Chick ventured out into the yard and pecked away at the seeds and bugs like everyone else.

Cock grew strong, beating off anything that threatened Chick. Mostly other roosters who just wanted to harass her and tease him. Cock walked a delicate balance with his brothers and cousins; being friends with them as long as they didn't try to accost Chick. No matter how you looked at it, his brothers and cousins treated him differently. He had crossed them and there's no going back from that.

Cock Rooster never forgot the feeling of being alone the day he watched Chick's birth. He did not miss any opportunity to explore this crazy feeling. He'd go off by himself, exploring. He'd check out the perimeter of the farm. One day, he found a way out. What lay before him appeared to be just a prairie; a prairie full of creatures great and small that dazzled his tiny bird brain. Many times Cock and Chick snuck out and played in the prairie field together.

One day some men came and watched the little roosters playing and fighting in the yard. Some of Cock's cousins liked the attention and showed off for the men. The men egged them on in their play and encouraged the little roosters to new levels of aggression. Not immune to peer pressure, Cock remembered what he was capable of after the dog incident when Chick was born.

The men intervened with the roosters knocking them around with their boots. They even hurt some of the roosters and watched their reactions. Some ran. Some roosters pulled away in pain and fear. Some got mad. Some became more aggressive. Cock got angry. He saw his cousins hurt badly and he lost his temper and he attacked one of the men. He pecked at the man and scratched at him with his sharp claws. The men cheered and laughed and knocked Cock around and hurt him. Cock went wild and attacked the man, this time, scratching and biting him. Finally the man grabbed Cock. He picked him up and held him close so Cock's wings folded under him. The man held Cock's head against his chest and spoke soft words to him; soothing him and petting him until Cock quit fighting and calmed down.

"There... There..." the man said.

All the other men circled around to look at Cock. He didn't resist as the men examined him. They put a red band around his leg and let him go.

Cock didn't calm down for hours.

The little scenario went on and on day after day. The same thing happened with some of the other roosters but only three got red bands around their legs.

The three banded roosters stood together and the others looked at them like they were aliens. This created an ugly scene.

Cock tried to peck off his band. He couldn't reach it. He pecked at his cousin's bands and they all joined in a team effort. No one wanted to be different and no one wanted anyone else to be different either. But sadly, the bands could not be pecked off.

Things flipped back to normal. As normal as could be expected with everyone starting at the red band around your leg. But roosters did what roosters do. They grew into preteens in rooster years. Things progressed as farm life does until one day some men came to the chicken coop and took all the young chickens … Chick among them. Upset, Cock followed her.

Distraught, Chick kept her eye on Cock. She watched as he went to the usual sneaky place they used to get in and out of the farm.

Cock followed Chick to a big white building. He walked around the building for hours until he saw Chick and they planned a way to get her out of there.

The men chased him back into the hen house.

Every day he snuck out of the farm. Every day Chick stood in the same place to meet him, in fact, she never moved. She watched him through a mesh part of the building. They looked at each other like the very first time they saw each other the day of Chick's birth.

Cock refined his plan. Moments away from carrying out his plan, men took him and his red-banded cousins to another building with only roosters. Cock found himself in a pen by himself. A pen he could not escape from. Cock liked to be alone but not alone like this cage.

The men gave him extravagant food and exercise. They bathed his feathers in strange liquids that smelled funny like lavender. He feasted on a staggering array of bugs.

The men allowed Cock to play with the other roosters. He had fun but the men teased them like they had done the first day in the henhouse. They teased, usually in playful fighting but sometimes things got rough and the men hurt the roosters and cheered once when another rooster hurt Cock.

Roosters that hurt other roosters garnished special attention from the men.

This went on and on day after day.

Cock noticed the roosters who lost it and injured another or hurt others disappeared. Cock thought maybe they had gone crazy and went to the loony bird bin. He didn't want to hurt the other roosters; they had become his friends, some his brothers, some his cousins, but Cock could only see Chick's face trapped in the big white building unable to move an inch. Leaving the pen for any reason could be a chance at escape; escape and a chance to carry out his plan to free Chick and run into the prairie field for whatever would befall them: life or death.

The next day during their aggressive play, one of Cock's cousins got so worked up he lost his mind and pecked Cock bad on the chest. His cousin went wild and pecked other cousins. A man immediately picked him up and took him out of the cockpit.

Out of his mind with pain and upset, like a chain reaction, Cock viciously attacked another cousin, knocked him down and pecked him until another man stopped him and returned them all to their separate cages.

This went on day after day. Great food. Great outdoor activity and fighting and hurting each other.

Before Cock knew what happened to him, he became a full-grown rooster: strong, muscular, healthy and beautiful. His bright eyes showed keen intelligence and his long multicolored feathers glowed in the dark.

Many of his brothers and cousins had been taken away. New roosters came into the pen. Cock had an easier time attacking the roosters he did not call friend or relative.

In the dark days of winter, the men matched Cock with a rooster he had never seen before with all black feathers. He was big. He was strong. He was mean.

Cock didn't know what hit him. He lost his temper big-time. Cock fought for his life. He didn't clearly remember what happened except he remembered the big, mean rooster cried out in pain. This time the men took Cock away. His big moment came. Carried by a handler; he watched and he waited and he took his first opportunity. He pecked the handler right by his eye. Maybe he picked him in the eye, he didn't know, but the man let him go and he escaped. He ran free.

A long time passed but he made it back to the henhouse and to the big white building. He had changed but Chick recognized him right away. She looked even more miserable then when he left.

A big, fat, ugly, smelly ranch hand caught Cock trying to free Chick and sent him back.

The men laid out even more royal treatment on Cock because he had the audacity to escape. His escape precipitated the inevitable to happen: the men sent him into the cockpit.

Many men stood around the arena. Many faces and bodies and smells and noises disoriented Cock and his heart beat in his chest like a rabbit's. They sent him to fight a kind of rooster he had never seen before. Vicious fighting ensued, but Cock lived ... only to do the same thing the next day. The easier it became for Cock to be violent with these other roosters that didn't look like his brothers and cousins, the worse he felt about himself. Cock hated to be forced to harm others but in the arena one law reigned supreme: kill or be killed. There's no getting around that.

One day, this is just what happened. Cock lost control. Even when the rooster he fought laid down Cock pecked him to death. He was treated like a king after that. He didn't even recognize himself. He killed many times. So many times. So many that one of the men took him home with him and Cock lived there. He lived right in the room with the man. The man pampered and petted him and he lived a life of luxury. He still went to the arena and still killed but now he liked it. He began to see himself as special. He never thought much about Chick.

At last the inevitable happened. Cock found himself in a fight to the death. A second from death; he lost. Paralyzed, Cock couldn't move at all. He couldn't move a feather. He could hear, though, and he heard his man declare him dead. His man tossed him out the back door into the garbage can. Other dead roosters laid under him. He heard one of the men say that Cock wasn't even good enough to eat. Cock's man went right to the winning rooster. He forgot Cock ever existed.

Cock rode to the dump in the garbage truck not knowing if he lived or had died. His man said he was dead so he must be dead. That's how screwy Cock's mind had become. The truck released its contents and Cock rolled down the hill with the other garbage. Buzzards flew around him. But they did not touch him. This is when Cock thought maybe he still lived. He watched the buzzards watching him. Soon it grew pitch black. Cock knew if he wasn't dead before he had to be dead now.

With the hazy morning sun, Cock made the slightest ever crow. He didn't even know he crowed. He crowed on reflex. The buzzards flew away. He knew he lived.

Seemed like days passed before Cock could flick bugs off himself with his wing. He scooted around to a more comfortable position. He flipped over and drank out of a mud puddle. Each night he looked into the eyes of the buzzards. He used to wish to be alone… but not like this. In fact, he felt so alone, the buzzards eyes watching him comforted him. At least they wanted him for something. The nights grew cold but when the sun came up each morning he made a stronger cock - a - doodle - do.

One day, the sun came up bright. Mellow yellow with an azure blue sky and Cock remembered Chick and the day of her birth. Her eyes blue like the sky and her fluffy feathers blazing yellow like the sun.

Cock got to his feet and headed to the farm; to Chick and to sure death. But Cock didn't care. He felt dead already. Maybe he lived. Maybe he dwelled somewhere in between like a ghost or something. But if he could look at her one more time he knew he'd be himself again and he could die happy.

Many days journey he traveled. Some areas he passed over produced an abundance of exotic bugs and seeds. Other areas lay barren for long stretches with no water. Day after day. He thought he'd die again out there alone, but he had a new alertness and cunning. He had a lust for life that he never had before. An abandon of sorts. The kind of zip one gets on their second life. He killed a lizard. He killed a sparrow. He drank from them. Each day he got stronger.

Miracles do happen. He made it to Chick. With many attempts he freed her from the pen that trapped her. Chick had been overfed. Her muscles had grown weak from nonuse. Cock had strength enough for both of them.

They ran into the prairie field and woods living in the wild by a clear stream. They climbed trees at night to get away from the nocturnal animals. They foraged during the day.

Chick slimmed down and got the strength back in her legs. They played together and ran together. Cock showed her many tricks he learned and the fancy things he could do with his body. Soon Chick played with him just like his brothers and cousins had done. They had a carefree time. They hardly had to go anywhere at all to get plenty of good bugs to eat and worms that they both considered a delicacy.

The stream water looked clear all the way to the bottom with many bugs laying around on the top like dragonflies. They bathed in the stream and their feathers grew beautiful. Their eyes shone clearly, the sun shined brightly, and they felt happiness like a new world.

They spent a lot of time playing around the stream. They loved to sit on the bank and roll in the sand but mainly they loved to look at each other. They had happy times living by that stream.

Soon they took turns sitting on Chick's eggs. They hatched into beautiful babies. Cock and Chick had four beautiful chiclets. All they did day after day was play, play, play. All too quickly, the chicks grew big enough to run superfast and get in a lot of trouble. This is when the fun really started.

One afternoon, all kinds of ruckus came from the woods. A flock of wild turkeys overran the area Cock and Chick called home. The size of the turkeys startled Cock at first, but the turkeys acted disorganized and nervous. Cock fought them to protect his territory. He soon saw his territory had been overrun. He discovered in a flash: territory wasn't all it was cracked up to be. Territory wasn't of any real importance to him. He'd do anything, though, to protect Chick and the chiclets.

Soon it became evident why the turkeys took off on the run. Hunters had come into the woods. Cock and Chick and the chiclets ran through the woods with the turkeys. The situation grew into a horrible deal. The hunters had no interest in Cock, Chick or the chiclets. The hunters took many turkeys by gunshot or traps. The turkeys that got away became panicked with fear. They went cuckoo and they couldn't organize themselves to fight but Cock and Chick fought the men.

Chick faught fearlessly. Chick fought like a savage. Chick pecked a man on his hands with ruthless abandon.

Cock threw his body out at them scratching them in the eyes. He puffed out his feathers and screeched so loudly the men covered their faces and their ears and ran away bleeding.

The remaining eight turkeys of different sizes and ages, Cock and Chick, and the two babies they had left, wandered off in disarray.

The turkeys acted crazy for days. Cock and Chick looked to be in not much better shape after bearing witness to two of their chicks carelessly trampled by the hunters. But they had two babies to take care of and that they did.

The remaining turkeys did not go territorial on Cock. The turkeys had bird brains, all right, but they were smart enough to know a good deal when they saw one. They made friends with Cock and Chick. Even though they both thought the other looked like the ugliest thing they'd ever seen, they banded together for safety, security, and camaraderie. The turkeys and the chickens had a lot in common. They had lived through a terrible war together. They wanted the same things; to sit on their eggs, hatch them, and watch their chicks grow.

Eight turkeys, Cock and Chick, and their two little ones followed the stream traveling deep into the woods. They traveled for days and days. They found a secluded inlet by the stream and a shallow cave and they settled there.

Cock gave the turkeys fighting lessons. He was an expert after all.

Many other birds came into the area. Some pheasants came with their feathers singed. The field they lived in had been burned out. Some babblers came from who knows where. Some love birds and some birds that had the longest legs anyone had ever seen but all they wanted to do was make a nest and sit. Some bird brains came from down south. They made the most God-awful noise; all the time, even worse than Cock crowing in the morning. They wanted to consume a bug now and then, play with their babies, and be safe at night.

A pair of beat-up yellow canaries showed up one day. They said their humans lost interest in them and carelessly left their cage open when cleaning it outside.

"We didn't know what to do! We didn't know what to do!" the canary chirped. "We ran into some old crows and they told us they were going to a merry cock and live free in a garden … a garden where a merry cock stands guard. They said we should come along too! We should come along too! Is this it? Is this it? Are you a merry cock? Are the crows here? We saw many other birds headed this way."

The canary sang the truth. Cock did perch himself up in a tree in the night and scan the area for intruders or anything dangerous that might come in the area. He did this all night every night. It made him happy. You could say he felt as happy as he could be.

Every morning, after he crowed uncontrollably, he'd relieve Chick and sit on their eggs for the day. Sitting all day after sitting all night irritated Cock but it made him happy to relieve Chick. Every time an egg cracked open and his little baby chick popped out he felt as happy as the first time he laid eyes on Chick. Every day more goofy birds came. As strange as seemed, that made him happy too. But to call him a merry cock… a merry cock … he never saw himself like that. They had traveled far from man. In the back of Cock's bird brain he knew man would catch up with them someday. He felt so happy he didn't care. You could say he was so happy he and Chick and the chiclets and all the looney birds lived happily ever after.

COMPLETE STRANGERS

By Lindsay Lake

Did you ever see the Hitchcock classic "Rear Window"? I live in a courtyard like that. Eight garages face each other, with the balcony above, overlooking the courtyard. The Courtyard of Woodside.

Cars zip in and out of the garages, people walk their dogs, kids play basketball and the little girl next to me scratches a big plastic car up and down the blacktop.

I imagine what my courtyard would look like from EarthCam or time-lapse; the garage doors opening and closing, the dusk-to-dawn light bulbs turning on and off, the peoples passionless scurry, like ants.

Sounds and smells drift in and out of my open window, bad classic rock radio, hip-hop; steaks grill, cigarette smoke and people talk on their cell phones.

We don't know each other. We wave when our cars pass. We say "Hi!" at the mailbox. What do I expect? Hey, it's the 21st-century. This is how it is. It's not that bad. When the chips are down, we band together and help each other..

During the blizzard of 2012 the men in the courtyard got up the next morning and shoveled out the 5-foot drifts blocking the garages of all the homes. I told the men they were my heroes. I had to work at the hospital at 3 p.m. and not everyone could make it in.

Last winter my neighbor's pipes broke, and his water flooded my garage. Another neighbor ran over to help with his shop vac.

Everyone is so into their own lives, including me, I don't know much about the lives that go on in the homes. All I know is what I can see from their garages. I don't know why people like to leave their garage doors open but they do. Personally, I don't want anyone to see my mess.

72

As in any neighborhood, there's always one guy, one yard that is immaculate, and puts everyone else to shame. That guy lives across from me to the left. You can have Sunday dinner on his garage floor, it's so clean. He has bike racks on the walls, a big screen TV, and a mosquito net that covers the whole garage door. Even his car has a cover. Imagine that. One day my garage is going to look like his; I swear.

Directly across from me is the complete opposite. This single mother and son have boxes from floor to ceiling in her garage with a little path to the door. Every winter I wonder why she doesn't move the boxes and park her car inside. After all, the garages are heated. But every year she struggles and scrapes the snow and ice from her windows and freezes; every summer she gets into her hot car and can't touch the steering wheel.

She is the only person in the courtyard that doesn't wave when the cars pass each other.

Once, she left her keys hanging out of her mailbox, which is right next to mine. I carried them to her door excited that after ten years of looking at each other I would get a chance to introduce myself and say hello. She didn't answer the door. I walked around the building and there her car sat in front of her open garage. I wrote a note. I wrapped the keys in the paper, put them in an envelope, and stuck the envelope under her windshield wiper.

I went about my business.

Sometime later her boy came to my door and said his ball had bounced onto my balcony and could I give it to him. Over the next five years or so, this same scene happened three more times at least. Sometimes, I would find a stray ball on my balcony when I went out for the sun in the morning. I threw the ball off the balcony in the direction of his garage. This is how we communicate with each other.

One time he came to my door for the ball, and I told him to be more careful, that he had grown up, that I wouldn't get the ball anymore or some such nonsense. I never saw the ball on my balcony again. I never saw him at my door again.

At night sometimes I hear her screaming at the boy like a banshee. She called him "stupid." She called him "lazy." She told him he didn't do what she told him to do. One time it got so bad I thought I should call somebody. I had a fantasy that he grew up and killed her. The police came to interview me, and I said what people usually say:

"Oh, he was the nicest boy. He never bothered anybody. No matter how much she yelled at him I never heard him say a thing."

Her screaming stopped when he outgrew her.

I whip my car around the corner into the courtyard and screech to a halt. The courtyard is full of cars and a huge moving van. The vans tires sunk into the soft immaculately landscaped grass leaving deep ridges a foot deep. I snake around the 98-gallon garbage cans and cars and trucks and five or six young men and make it into my garage. The men carry all the boxes from my neighbors garage into the van.

"Oh," I say to myself. "She's rented a storage bin!" I walk in my house and do the things one usually does.

I take a crummy old hotdog out of the refrigerator, roll it in a corn tortilla, and eat my dinner over the sink.

I glance a few times out the window. Her garage is empty. I can't explain how beautiful that looks.

The next time I look out, the men are moving furniture into the van.

"That's odd." I say out loud, and I call it a day.

The open window is a blessing. I can hear the activity from the protected wetlands on my right. I hear the birds and crickets and frogs. I hear the Canadian geese sail in like large duck dinners tantalizing the nocturnal carnivores in the area.

The next morning the sun streams in my window and I feel as laid up as Jimmy Stewart. I look out the window,

74

and she's gone. Her house is empty.

I don't think much about it but every time I glance out my window I hear nothing. I see nothing. Her windows stare back at me like two black eyes with the garage its empty mouth.

CORDA QUAERENTIUM

By S. Houk

Watch what your heart desires.
What you seek in the daytime,
You will seek when you aren't looking.
In the unguarded moment,
In the middle of a stolen night -
One more night than you were supposed to have -
Your heart will wake up early
With the Roar of your Daytime
To wake the mountains
To wake the jungle
To wake the prairie
To wake the abyss.
When you aren't looking
It will win.

CRACKS

By S. Houk

Cracks don't happen slowly. They pop
On a cold day
Right across the windshield.
Then you watch it find its way
Like water
Through a tiny gap -
A long fissure
Keeping dinosaurs on one side.

Things don't uncrack.

Maybe you take the windshield
And grind it up
To molecules
That are cracked.

Maybe you take the windshield
And melt it in fire
To a glob
That is cracked.

Maybe you fill up the fissure
With dead dinosaurs.

Maybe you blacken the windshield
And drive on through the night.

Maybe you kick the windshield out
Like a "don't drown" video.

Maybe

Maybe you ride your dinosaurs

Up out of the Grand Canyon
Across a few ice ages
And sit them right down to dinner.
Drink a glass of wine, dinos.
We are not done here yet.

DARK PROTECTOR: A DARAGA EXCEERPT

By Colleen H. Robbins

Sandy Hook, southernmost city in the East

The noise of the marketplace nearly overwhelmed her. Not the physical noise, though the smith hammering out small repairs on his portable anvil throbbed in time with her burgeoning headache, but the mental noise beneath the dickering.

Raisa could usually block out the constant mental hum, but the anger/ glee/ excitement/ triumph in the thoughts around her amplified everything. She rubbed her fingers in a circular motion on her temples and pinched the pointed tips of her ears twice before hiding them beneath her hair, then went through the mental steps to raise her shields. She relaxed as the noise faded into the background.

Glancing at a tented booth of carvings--one of only three run by elves at this Gathering marketplace--she recognized the code for a Yarite rendezvous in the braided ribbons adorning the corner poles. Finally, a chance to redeem herself.

An angry shout--a mental voice she recognized--slid right through her shields and echoed inside her head, followed by screams both mental and physical. Raisa ducked around a cloth merchant's booth and peeked back between bolts of cloth. The two-story towers of the sprawling castle on the hill could be seen above the multicolored tents that filled the street. Hundreds of shoppers crowded around. A tall warrior moved in the distance. She focused on his face, the features magnifying enough to recognize him.

Damn, she thought. *Perok is still on my trail. Doesn't the jerk know when to give up?*

Apparently not. She darted through a knot of humans, thankful for once that her unusually tanned skin and light brown hair blended so well with theirs. Dressed in leather pants and a vest with her weapons sheathed, she might be mistaken for a man if it weren't for her long hair. Perok's voice--physical and mental--grew closer. She ran two steps and skidded into a narrow alley. Garbage along the left wall, long shadows in the back, and a heap of filthy rags halfway down the right side. She headed for the rags. Three steps before she reached them, the rags rustled and something sat up. Raisa lost the rhythm of her steps and veered to the left, heart pounding. Rounding the back corner of the building, she slid on rotting fruit peels and ran full-face into a wall. She slapped the wall in reflex, saving her face from scrapes, but making far too much noise. Her nose wrinkled. The sharp lime scent of the fresh mortar smelled almost as bad as the garbage. She crouched in the shadows of the shallow alcove, fumes soaking into her clothes and hair. She could never appear at the evening rendezvous like this.

"Raisa, wait!" Perok's voice echoed along the street. Raisa could visualize his progress, pushing people out of his path as though they barely existed.

"Hey, stop pushing!" Raisa felt the victim's outrage before she heard the words. She brought her mental shields up to full. She had never seen inside Perok's mind, and she did not want to. His stray thoughts unsettled her enough with untampered bloody images.

She once kissed Perok to distract him and save her brother's life. Perok's comments before the kiss were those of a boy trying to seduce a girl; afterward his father Garag's letters attested to the seriousness of his proposal.

She might have considered it if Perok had not been dangerously insane.

The rustle grew louder, and Raisa peeked around the corner. The alley lit up in wavering colors. *Not again*, she thought. *It's been six months. How much longer will the* likshas *affect me?* The odd colors gave everything an unnatural appearance.

A filth-encrusted madwoman rushed to the mouth of the alley, leaving a trail of rags behind and gabbling wildly at a terrified young woman. With a start, Raisa realized that she understood a few of the words. Where had the madwoman learned the Melani tongue?

Curious now, Raisa focused on the madwoman's return to the alley, defeat written in the stooped shoulders and downcast gaze as the woman picked her rags up one by one. The unnatural

80

glow in the alley faded, revealing the woman's true colors. Her dark skin hung in blue-black wrinkles and folds except where it stretched around the lumpy tumors common to those who spent a lifetime working in the sun. Even from twenty feet away, Raisa could tell that the woman did not have long to live.

The woman's hair retained its dark color in spite of her apparent age. It hung past her waist, ragged and uneven when not completely matted. She took a deep breath, stood, and flung her head back in a surprisingly regal gesture. Her tangled hair flipped up, revealing a glimpse of pointed ears even taller than Raisa's before it fell back across her face.

Raisa stepped back in shock. The madwoman was a dark-skinned, dark-haired elf? What was a Melani elf doing *here*, in a human city?

The woman darted out again, this time accosting Perok and gabbling at him.

Perok's shoulder-length hair swung loose, just a few shades darker than Raisa's light brown. At eighteen, he stood tall for a human, taller than his father and a handbreadth taller than Raisa. Lips drawn up in a snarl, he clubbed the woman to the ground with his fist and kicked at her as she tried to roll away.

Raisa flexed her fingers next to the hilt of a throwing knife. She would have pegged a stranger to the wall, but Perok ran with the group of young men her brother Nicholas called friends. She forced her fingers to relax. Growing more irritated at being trapped while Perok took out his frustration on the old woman, yet not willing to draw his attention, Raisa closed her eyes against the sight and sounds of the beating and kept her mental shields shut tight.

I ought to feel something for the woman, she thought. *My sister would. Pity? Anger?* She mentally shrugged. *I feel nothing.*

Sandy Hook

The noises from the alley mouth stopped, save for an occasional groan from the madwoman. Raisa remained out of sight. Six months' absence should have been enough to cool Perok's passion for her. It certainly cooled her passion for the Yarites. *Betrayers.*

81

The madwoman's voice rose again. Curious, Raisa watched as the old Melani elf crawled to the street and begged for assistance. The passing humans ignored her. Raisa could understand why: they did not understand what she asked. Even if they could, they would likely have ignored her anyway. It was the way the world thought, even if they sometimes acted differently. Raisa stepped from the shadows at the back of the alley.

The Melani woman extended a rag-covered arm, hand palm up. "I beg, I beg you to help me. I must find the Bride. Only she can rescue my daughter." The woman's Melani, perfectly accented, wavered between the tenses of a high-born and those of a servant. Light flashed from a tarnished silver slave bracelet almost hidden beneath her rags.

What an odd combination. The accent was more difficult to learn than the tenses.

"I must find the Bride," the Melani woman repeated.

Raisa tilted her head. Did the woman fall from a high rank to a low? Was the tense shift brought on by homelessness? Curiosity won. "Tell me who you seek." Raisa kept her voice neutral of emotion, her tense indicating her high birth. As the daughter of ambassadors, she ranked just beneath the children of the Eastern kings.

"Sun-God be praised! You understand my words!" The madwoman crawled to Raisa's feet, laying her head to the side in a submissive gesture.

"Yes, I understand your words. Tell me who you seek." Raisa added a note of command this time. If the Yarites did not already know of her arrival from Perok's shouting, she had little time to leave before their meeting. Attending when she smelled like this would be a mortal insult.

"I seek the Bride of the Khensu, the Death-Bringer. Only she can help me find my daughter." A note of urgency crept into the woman's voice.

"Who is this Death-Bringer?"

The Melani woman's face grew animated beneath her wrinkles, though her voice lowered to a respectful hush. "The Death-Bringer Shess once a Life-Bringer sent to find a sacrifice for the Sun-God. He succeeded and brought back an elf of light, one

82

who might return the Sun-God's favor. But when Shess returned, his touch brought death to those around him." The Melani looked down and shuddered violently.

An assassin? No, something else.

The Melani looked up at Raisa with intense yellow eyes. "The Bride, she defied the Death-Bringer and struck him on the third day of their wedding. She used her magics to escape and the Death-Bringer's own men killed him. I escaped to the upper world in the confusion and came to this land."

Raisa nodded thoughtfully. No wonder the woman went mad. If even half her tale was true... "How long ago did this happen?"

"Almost seventeen years past. The sailor who brought me here took me to wife. He gave our daughter Vani the best of everything. Two years ago, an evil spirit possessed my husband. He sold Vani and me to slavers. I ran away and have looked for Vani ever since. When I came here, I saw the Bride pass in the distance. She did not hear my calls. She can help me."

"Tell me more of this Bride." *If she is powerful enough,* thought Raisa, *perhaps she can help me get rid of Perok's attentions.*

"She is *elf.*" The Melani woman spat the word out like a curse. "She is favored of the Sun-god. Her hair is the color of the sun and her eyes are the color of the sky."

"There are many who look so, including my brother." *My whole family,* thought Raisa. *I am the only one different. Born ten minutes before the other two, I am the one who must have a different father.*

The Melani woman scrutinized Raisa's face, timidly reaching out to lift the girl's hair and stare at her ears. "You are also elf, I see." The word held no curse in it this time. Urgency crossed the madwoman's face and her eyes became wild. "You must help me find her! I must find the Bride to save my daughter!"

Still curious, Raisa lowered her shields partway. Images seeped across the barrier. "You have described many. Does the Bride have a name?"

The Melani woman frowned, then nodded. She dropped her voice to a whisper. "The Bride of the Death-Bringer, the sun-favored elf, she who called herself Timbrel."

Raisa stumbled backward, nearly falling across a heap of garbage. Her mother's image pulsed in her thoughts.

The old Melani woman tentatively reached out a gnarled hand. "Do you know where I can find the Bride?"

Raisa recovered, though her speech faltered. "I know where Timbrel is. How can my mo..." She paused and corrected herself. "How can the Bride help you?"

"She will keep my daughter safe with her magics. Melani warriors stalk the streets at night wearing rival colors. One called my name. Two of them carried death daggers, blades smeared with black poison and the hilts wrapped with red ribbon. They would cut our throats so that the Redvee clan will die out and the songs will be lost."

Raisa, Timbrel's daughter, stood and dropped her right hand to the hilt of her sword. Something felt out of place. Was that a soft scuff against the stone of the emptying street? Did she hear a whisper of her name? The alley they stood in dead-ended at the new wall, potentially trapping them. They had to move quickly.

She used her left hand to steer the Melani woman toward the street.

"She fought against the Death-Bringer. The Bride possesses great magic. She will keep my daughter safe."

Raisa glanced out of the alley at the shadowed street. The sun balanced on the horizon. Those with honest business were already home, and those without such were not yet out. Raisa sniffed her clothes. She would not go to the rendezvous tonight. The Three-Horse Inn stood a block and a half away. The barred doors and windows would provide safety. "Come with me. We'll spend the night at the inn, then tomorrow we'll leave on my boat and you can tell me more about the Bride." *And about Khensu Shess*. They rounded a corner. Raisa heard footsteps--or their echoes--in the distance. She bent over without warning to touch her boot lace. There. One last step. She risked a glance and caught a flicker of movement.

"Run. Now!" She grabbed the Melani woman's hand and half-dragged her to the inn. Running steps sounded in the distance. Raisa pulled her inside and slammed the door.

Their entrance drew unwanted attention. Raisa memorized the faces in the room with a quick glance. If any followed her later, she would recognize them. She wiped her hand on her thigh, fingers slightly separated into pairs. The innkeeper nodded as he lifted his smallest finger off the bar. Guiding the old woman upstairs, Raisa turned left and walked to the end of the short hallway. A door led into a small but oddly shaped room filled with brooms and baskets of supplies.

"Where are we going?" The Melani woman's voice rose in pitch.

"To a place of safety." Raisa jerked her around the corner as footsteps came up the hallway. She pushed the row of cloaks hanging there aside and pressed on the wall. A small door popped open. Grabbing a jar of softened soap, she pulled the Melani inside a hidden closet and bolted the door securely behind them. Loud knocking echoed in the halls, followed by the crash of a broken door.

Raisa and the woman sat quietly as voices raised below and an argument ensued. They could hear the shouts of the city guard approaching from the street. After more running feet and raised voices, Raisa listened to the sound of the guards leaving, their prisoner's protestations fading with distance.

When all grew quiet, she sat next to the Melani woman. She leaned over and whispered. "How did you meet the Bride?"

The Melani woman lifted her head proudly. "When I was young like you, seventeen years ago, I served the Bride and prepared her for her wedding. I helped make her dress from black spider silk stiffened with *yenu*."

Raisa did not recognize the word, but let the woman ramble on about the wedding preparations for a few minutes while they washed the worst of the stink off in a bucket of stagnant water in the corner.

"I think I can help you. What is your true name, fallen lady?" Raisa used the most respectful term she could to indicate her understanding. The Melani language had few terms of respect for a higher to use towards a lower caste.

"I am Vanisi, once servant to the Bride, once wife to Kadeesh the merchant, and daughter of Valain of the House of Redvee."

Raisa nodded acknowledgement. "I am Raisa, warrior-trained and daughter to Timbrel, whom you call the Bride."

Sandy Hook

Vanisi drew backwards, then crept forward again. She slowly reached out to stroke a thin finger against Raisa's face, and then along her long ear. "It could be. You have your mother's look to you." Vanisi ran her fingers through Raisa's hair. The light brown seemed almost blonde against the woman's palm. "Your hair is light, but so is your mother's. You look the right age."

The intense scrutiny disturbed Raisa. "The right age for what?"

Vanisi's sagging face came within inches of Raisa's. "Before he died, the Khensu Shess, the Death-Bringer, spent two nights with the Bride. You could be his daughter. Are you born in the spring?"

Raisa froze, unable to speak. She had always felt different than her siblings. Perhaps Vanisi could tell her more. "I. . . I was. How did you know?"

"I left in the confusion when the Death-Bringer died. I birthed Vani in late spring."

The next morning, Sandy Hook, the Three Horse Inn

Raisa woke to the yeasty smell of rising bread from the kitchens below. Pinkish pre-dawn half-light glowed between the boards of the outer wall.

Vanisi, already awake, watched Raisa through amber eyes. "Is it time?" she whispered.

Raisa nodded. Carefully unbolting the door, she listened for a moment before opening it. The two eased their way through the storeroom, avoiding overturned buckets and broken brooms. Raisa grabbed a piece of ragged oilskin and tucked it into her harness. A few minutes later, they dodged freshly hung laundry in the inn's side yard, crept past the washer-women at their trough near the well, and slipped into the alley beyond.

Raisa led the way through the deserted back streets of Sandy Hook, streets she knew even better than the port city's waters. In an hour they would be at the docks, ready to sail north and search for Vanisi's daughter.

Her ears twitched like a cat at the faintest scuff of leather on stone. Were they followed already? Or had they wandered into someone else's trap?

Motioning for Vanisi to hide in the nearest alley, Raisa circled back. A slender man with a crossbow stalked slowly up the street, kneeling occasionally to check for signs. She ran through her memory and recognized him: one of Arlis' newer Yarite trainees.

Another fuzzy memory surfaced, this time her own: Arlis assigned by Master Celiar to train her in striking vital organs. Her reward, a sip from the Yarite cup. Waking after a blackout with Arlis in the same bed. Anger flooded through her as the rest of the memory woke. The Yarites had drugged her and used her. *Betrayers*!

A crossbow bolt shattered on the wall behind her. Raisa startled and flashed a hand sign identifying herself as a Yarite; the student cocked his bow, readying a second shot. She twisted away, wide-eyed, angry at herself for losing focus. He sprinted after her.

She twisted and turned through narrow alleys, scooping up some small broken jars. She ducked into a recessed doorway and chucked a jar to the far end of the alley just before her pursuer skidded around the corner. He stood framed against the dawn sky for just a moment. The jar bounced off the back wall and shattered into a pile of pottery pieces. The student ran past Raisa's hiding place.

She stepped out, slashing across his kidneys from behind. "Stupid, stupid, stupid," she muttered. The young Yarite turned his head as he crumpled to the ground, mouth still rounded in an 'o' of surprise. "Arlis should have trained you better. Sloppy work." She stepped around the growing pool of steaming blood. Raisa searched his body quickly, concentrating on the pouches hanging from his belt and wary of hidden needles. She pocketed a set of throwing daggers and two small bits of parchment. Abandoning the crossbow, she tucked his weighty money pouch into her tunic and wedged it between her breasts. She wiped her blade clean on the student's pants, then slipped away through the alleys to rejoin Vanisi.

The alley was empty, a few rags leading toward the alley's mouth. The soft glow returned. Barely visible against the colors of the garbage, a slightly lighter color led from the rags, out of the alley, and down the block to another alley. With no other clue, Raisa followed the fading path. The glow faded completely.

The silence alerted her as she approached the second alley. No flutter of crows. No scritching of mice and rats foraging in the garbage. The coppery odor of blood hung heavy in the air. Raisa whirled into the entrance, her dagger in hand, and covered half the length of the alley before she drew two breaths. Two dark-skinned figures fled the opposite end, but not before she identified them as Melani warriors. Raisa slowed as she passed a garbage heap.

Vanisi knelt behind the garbage, one hand grasping her throat. She used the other to motion Raisa closer. Blood oozed between her clenched fingers.

Vanisi's voice was no more than a bubbling whisper, forcing Raisa to drop her shields and listen to the Melani's mind as well as her words.

"You must find my daughter Vani! She is in danger! They hunt the Redvee clan. Vani, daughter of Vanisi, is the last singer." Blood streamed freely between Vanisi's fingers now, and flecks of blood dotted her lips.

Raisa reached for Vanisi's shoulder. "Quiet yourself. We will find a healer."

The old woman's eyes blazed amber and she struggled to sit upright. "I am Vanisi, daughter of Valain Redvee. Find and protect my daughter Vani." The last word came out accompanied by a bubble of blood. She took a final gurgling breath and threw her arms wide. Blood fountained from her throat, covering Raisa in hot crimson as her words burrowed into Raisa's mind.

88

Raisa threw up her mental shields, but too late. The words rang through her mind again and again. "Find and protect Vani." They became a chant, matching Raisa's breathing and heartbeat, suffusing her being.

Timbrel's daughter staggered back, dripping with Vanisi's blood. The woman's throat had been cut so deeply that Raisa could almost see her spine. Vanisi had clung to life, holding her own throat together, just to give her dying command.

Raisa bent her head in respect. Such a strong spirit would no doubt watch over her as she completed its mission. The words echoing over and over in her mind gave her no other option.

Shassilar, where all roads meet in the East, home of the Wizard Haz

Vani stood from polishing the floor, set her rag aside, then added water to the kettle of stew. She laid the lid against the hearth while she stirred, then swung the kettle back over the corner of the fireplace to continue heating uncovered.

A thumb-sized flame hopped across the coals like a flame-red lizard in pursuit of coal black insects, leaving new flames in its wake. Humming to herself, Vani hopped from one foot to the other, then stirred the stew again and picked up her rag again to polish the wax into the next section of dark grey flagstone floor. She did not know the fire stirred itself behind her. Ashes fell and bright flames merrily danced beneath the kettle. The smell of bubbling stew filled the room.

"Are you done yet, girl? We must cover the black stone before *he* sees me." Haz's voice faded to faint mumblings from the next room.

Vani set the rag and wax aside and scurried across the room to the wooden bucket where a stained tablecloth soaked in bleach-water. *This will never be white again*, she thought. *The old wizard is senile. He expects the impossible from me.*

Vani sighed and scrubbed at the cloth. The fumes stung her nose and eyes. Circular red bleach spatters marred the nut-brown skin on her arms and the tarnished silver bracelets that adorned her wrists. Why any other tablecloth would not do to cover the black stone square inset in the ancient metal table, she would never understand. The old wizard remained convinced that the square stone would send images to a rival wizard. In the two years Vani served Haz, the stone did nothing but reflect the room when she polished it every morning. The wizard swore he heard voices from the stone.

Vani whispered part of a jump rope rhyme from her free years. "They blew apart whatever they had. All the wizards went mad." Haz certainly was.

The kitchen door slammed open and Simon skidded into the room. He careened wildly across the freshly waxed floor, crashing into a table. A green ceramic jar teetered on the edge. Vani reached out as the jar fell just beyond her outstretched fingers, smashing on the floor and scattering dozens of finger-length leaves.

"Simon!" Haz would probably punish *her* for Simon's mistake. The boy apprentice could do no wrong in the wizard's eyes. As Vani quickly found out after Haz purchased her, eight-year-old boys could manage to get into quite a bit of trouble.

Simon scooped up the green shards, his eyes downcast. "I'm sorry, Vani. I'll get them." He carefully picked up three leaves.

Vani snorted, returning to the tablecloth. The stains looked a little lighter.

Simon threw open the shuttered window. The breeze curled inside, scattering the leaves further. Before Vani could say anything, Simon scrunched up his face in a vicious-looking squint, crossed his eyes, and stared out the window. The neighbor's servant squawked in outrage and shook her rake at the boy.

Vani rushed over to pull him back inside. Simon glared at her and started whispering, then ran over to an empty glass jar and poked the three leaves inside. Now that she could hear him a little better, Vani realized that some of his words were similar to the Melani tongue she learned from her mother.

"I... going... win," Simon whispered. "I... more leaves."

Vani looked around. There was no one else nearby. Did Simon speak with ghosts?

The wind swirled around the room, spinning the leaves into the air in a miniature whirlwind. The whirlwind settled over the jar, dropping the leaves inside. Simon clapped his hands and laughed, then whispered something else. Miniature thunder cracked and the breeze reversed, blowing back out the window. Vani hurried to close the shutters.

"See? All picked up." The boy sounded pleased with himself.

"By a ghost." Vani shivered and edged away from him. "How did you do that?"

"It wasn't a ghost!" Simon yelled. His face turned red, then faded back to his normal tan. "It's just a little animal. They hide in air, fire, water, and even the ground. The four elements." He shyly glanced up at Vani. "You think I'm crazy, don't you? That's why my father sent me here, you know. A crazy apprentice for a crazy wizard." He frowned and spat on the floor.

Vani paused in her scrubbing. She looked at the spot on the floor and arched an eyebrow. Simon looked back at the spot in the middle of the polished floor. His ears turned red, then he grabbed a rag from the table and wiped it up.

"I've never seen any animals in the fire unless they were roasting on a spit." Vani scrubbed again at the cloth. She held it up, the stains somewhat faded. She laid the broomstick between the table and the counter and draped the tablecloth across to dry.

"You have to look at them the right way. Mostly they're invisible." Simon glanced around quickly and lowered his voice. "Promise you won't tell Haz?"

"I promise." Vani wondered about the boy's sanity. Trying to look anywhere else, her gaze fell on the jar of leaves. Something *had* lifted them. "So... How do I look for invisible animals?"

"You're just making fun of me." Simon pouted, his lower lip curling down so far it almost touched his chin.

Vani stifled a giggle. "No, really, I want to know."

Simon stared at her suspiciously from the side of his eye, then slowly brightened to a tentative smile. "Well, okay. Hold your hands out in front of you and spread your fingers."

Vani put her hands up in front of her face. "You didn't have *your* hands up."

"I don't need to anymore. I've been practicing. Stretch out your arms."

Vani stretched her arms out, knocking over a bowl of lentils. She glanced at the spilled beans, then frowned at Simon.

"Now, look at your hands, and then look at the wall past them. Pull your hands slowly in until they're close to your face. What do you see?"

"The most horrible fingernails I've ever seen. They're ragged!" She tucked her hands under her arms.

"You're not supposed to look at your *hands*. You're supposed to look *past* them. They should be kind of blurry. Try again."

Vani put her hands out again. *This better not be a joke.* She pulled her hands in slowly, and started again twice before she stopped focusing on her hands when they grew near. *They did look blurry.* She pulled them a few inches closer. "Hey, I can see through my fingers. They're like ghosts."

"Good. Now don't move your eyes. Look around very slowly. No, I said *don't* move your eyes."

"How am I supposed to look if I don't. . . Oh, wait. I see green specks in the air and some green flames in the hearth."

"You found them! Now come look outside the window."

Vani blinked to get her eyes back into focus and started toward the window. She blinked again, letting her eyes go out of focus. The green specks floated next to her. "Simon, do I have to use my hands? I can see the green things without them."

Simon whirled around, his mouth open and his eyes welling with tears. "That's *not* fair. I had to practice and you *didn't*? It's not *fair!*"

"Hush, you'll bother Haz."

Simon quieted, then pretended to stomp silently across the floor.

Vani hummed as she stared out the workroom window, ignoring the mess behind her. She let her vision go out of focus. Almost immediately she noticed the stirring of dust motes in the air. Looking more directly at the creature, it took on a faintly iridescent green glow. After she saw the first, the others appeared everywhere. One struggled in a puddle left after the recent rains. A

92

handful more worked their way just below the surface of the ground like small green worms, pulsing forward and contracting their tails as they moved across the small yard between the wizard's house and the neighbor's bushes.

The dust motes of the air elemental drifted from a spherical cloud to a pair of four foot tall butterfly-like wings. For a moment she thought she saw a faerie. The elemental hung in the air, wings rippling steadily, reminding Vani of a breeze blowing across a lake.

"Come here, come here," she whispered in Melani. Rippling her fingers to attract its attention, Vani tried to coax the elemental to the window. She wanted to try Simon's trick of "playing games" with the creature and get it to pick up the bowl of dried lentils she knocked over.

"Vani, no!" Simon's horrified voice startled both Vani and the elemental. Simon dove at her legs and knocked her from the window. She glimpsed the angry elemental, swirling into a whirlwind outside the window, just before Simon slammed the shutters closed and latched them. The swirl loomed up far larger than she anticipated.

The wind howled and shook the walls. Jars and baskets tumbled from the table. The howling grew louder and took on an angry tone. Vani and Simon huddled together. The roof thatch lifted in places. Cold wind swirled into the room. Baskets and curtains flapped in the breeze, then plummeted to the floor like so many hailstones as the elemental seemed to lose interest. It floated away before they spoke.

"What went wrong?" Vani whispered.

"You should only play with the little ones." Simon held his hands a few inches apart. "The big ones are too strong."

Vani nodded. Simon was wise beyond his eight years. "I will remember that," she promised.

Simon looked around the room. "We should pick this up before. . . "

Haz stormed into the room yelling. "What are you brats doing?" Haz's white hair stuck out from the sides of his head, and green and red stains marred the tip of his beard. He turned his head slowly. Baskets and jars were dumped everywhere. A bucket rolled in the corner. The worktable lay on its side. The curtains hung in tatters. The black stone gleamed in the metal table; the only object not moved by the elemental's fury.

"No!" The wizard made an arthritic dive across the room and grabbed the stained tablecloth. "The enemy can see us. Quick! Cover the stone." He flung the cloth toward Vani.

It fell short. She picked her way past overturned furniture to retrieve it. Haz struggled to stand, hands planted firmly on the floor while he tried to straighten his legs.

Vani shook the damp cloth out while Simon brushed a few stray leaves from the black stone. At his touch, it flared to life.

FINDING HOME

Katie Ward

Helping a person find his way home seems an easy enough task, especially when that person is your husband. Contrary to that notion, however, it seems that my efforts to do just that turned out to be an insurmountable challenge.

Let me explain:
Chris had been a long time on his Alzheimer's journey, and I was along for the ride acting variously as travel companion, guide, and apparently as a clueless navigator as well. Indeed, despite the fact that he/I/we had already met a number of potholes along the road, the mistake that I made was a sinkhole, a sinkhole that started right in our family room.

One late afternoon Chris sat on our sofa, right ankle resting on his left knee looking for all the world like a man perfectly at peace with the world. I was feeling at peace too because I could see him and knew that he was not wandering or getting into any predicaments. The peace was broken, however, when he abruptly announced that he needed transportation. We had some time previously managed to traverse the no-more-driving territory, so I said "Sure, where do you want to go?"

His reply stunned me.
When he answered that he needed to go home, I should have at least had an inkling that this was an altogether new development on the journey. He wanted to go home, I thought? He was in our family room, and he wanted to go home?!! What was needed at this point was a flashing neon sign reading "Warning! Warning!" But of course, there was nothing of the kind.

I blundered on blindly.
With no idea how to find home for him, and not realizing that I was making an enormous mistake, one that took us off road

altogether, I immediately brainstormed what seemed to be the perfect answer. Grabbing a fairly recent family photo, I showed him the backyard, the river, the and the whole family. I named the four grown kids. Their spouses. The eleven grands. Surely that would help him to recognize home. Right?!

Not so much....

His response to seeing the photo and listening to me blabber on with all the names was completely unexpected. And at that point in his Alzheimer's journey, his reaction was unprecedented. Instead of being calmed and finding some recognition in the photo, Chris exhibited immediate and exaggerated agitation. At this point, I was washed over by the awful awareness that he not only didn't recognize that he was in his own home, but that he didn't recognize me either.

What to do then?

I had no map, no GPS to help him to find home or to inform me how in the world I could help him. Clearly he didn't recognize or want THIS home; that was a certainty. Maybe he wanted his childhood home? Or maybe the home where our children were born and grew up? Or maybe another?

Off we set - hapless wanderers trying to find home..

Having no clue and only a hope that one of these must be the home that he knew and needed so greatly, I determined that we simply had to go and find which one it was. Undoubtedly one of those places would quell his state of agitation. In desperation, I loaded him into the car that he loved but could no longer drive, and off we headed to find home. Little did I know that it would be the first of countless trips on that same quest. Nor was even one of the expeditions meant to end in finding the elusive "home."

Midnight trips were made driving to May Street where he grew up with his Mom and brothers and his often absent father, the small two bedroom ranch in Joliet where so much love and so much pain existed together. But May Street was clearly not the home that Chris had in mind. Not at all.

Similarly, we tried to find home for him at Manor Court, his grandmother's home. That corner brick home was where he and his brothers and his cousins grew up together for years in the shadow of his deceased but not forgotten powerful grandfather, the one whose multiple kidnappings loomed powerfully in the collective memory of the family. But just like May Street, Manor Court was not home. It was not a place of refuge for Chris now. No place seemed to assuage the anxiety that Chris demonstrated, the desperation he felt and that could only be relieved by "going home."

Nevertheless, I kept on trying. Maybe home was Cassie Drive where we raised our family in a loving neighborhood, the two blocks long street that existed as part of a proverbial village that raised our children and many others. Nope! That wasn't home either.

Would Lockport be home?

I just needed to find a way to lessen his increasing agitation, to keep him from attempting to jump out of the car again. I'd drive to Lockport. We passed the two story corner house, the one where we raised the teenagers, where we held wedding celebrations for them. And we passed the schools where he had loomed so large as their leader; where he had led with integrity and good humor. Surely home was that community where he was loved and honored. Would that be home? Maybe there? Surely there?

Wrong again! And again and again. Then when I ran out of places to find "home" the real panic came - my own. The man who had calmly managed any number of crises became even more upset that I wasn't taking him home. We'd been driving a long time and he still wasn't home. He became convinced that a perfect stranger (me) was taking him AWAY from home. I had no more ideas. Nowhere else to drive. The choices had been exhausted.
......

Then finally the answer came!

My own sense of desperation waned as I realized that "home" was not a place at all, not a structure, not a community, not any of the things that my non-Alzheimer's mind thought it was.

No, instead "home" was a feeling.

Home was a feeling of being safe. It was a place that couldn't exist for a brain that couldn't recognize anything, or any place, or anyone. It was a feeling of familiarity and security. It was the feeling that a person has upon returning home after a long time away, finding himself once again in a world that he could navigate in the dark, a place where no address is needed, a place where a GPS system would be worthless. (Maybe unneeded rather than worthless?)

Home was a feeling, and I would never be able to drive him to it. Home was a feeling that would only now and then return to him unannounced. A gift. Like homes are. And a gift to me as well, not something I could ever find, no matter how hard I tried. To understand that was to accept that I could never make things better. I could only be there to help him search. And though his quest mostly continued, we were still able to find a few smooth roads to travel along the way.

FINGERING THE TUNE

By Duanne Walton

The porky broad flapped her gums about getting stuck in a romantic comedy, but I wasn't givin' her no mind. My meat was the tune playin' underneath her yap. Some dame singing, "Dibby, dibby, dip-dip-dip. Aaaa-aaah!" I'd heard it before, but couldn't finger the moniker.

Time for some gumshoeing. Cue Peter Gunn.

Mancini? Anthony? Blues Brothers? Let's get kooky and go with Art of Noise.

Too bad my fedora disappeared into the black hole of my storage unit.

I had a couple leads.

Someone claimed the tune was by some dame named Minaj. I tracked down the video on the tube of me. While stupefied by the shiny fabric billowing in the fan blowing, I realized this wasn't what I was after. The video I remembered had a broad with scary hair surrounded by ginks dressed as ballerinas.

The video I was looking for got mocked by these two palookas from a way back. They were kind of a guilty pleasure of mine. Saps, but they knew how to bust a gut. Nobody knew from nothing their parents, their real monikers, or if they were even human. Everyone just called them Beavis & Butthead.

Found them in the same dump they'd always been in. Parking their keisters on the same fleabag couch, watching the same TV. Butthead made a lame gasser about Mickey divorcing Minnie because she was "doin' Goofy."

The only Goofy ones here were them!

His compadre spilled about a tune called, "From a Distance." Boy, the chin music that could've been played on him! He was a whole orchestra!

I dug up the video and that wasn't it. God *is* watching us, though.

Finally I stumbled across a list of every single comment they made on every single video they watched. I took a deep breath and dove in, searching for the one with Butthead's "doin' Goofy" line.

And I fingered the tune.

No More "I Love You's" by Annie Lennox. The same dame that told me what sweet dreams were made of and when the rain was coming again, back when her hairstyle was better.

And it was *her* tune that played under the fat broad's gum flapping, not Minaj. Minaj had this clicking/finger snapping in hers, Lennox didn't.

Case closed. I could now resume my regularly scheduled life.

FIBER OPTIMIST

By James Moore

Friends I so implore you
now please quit this bad habit
for the meals you consume
ought look more like a rabbit's

your daily food intake
truly lacking in roughage
a cause of grief and pain
bad intestinal stuffage

it makes one to be mean
the grumbling grouch who will growl
he who's heart is burdened
by slight or no movement of bowel

some may beg the question
about the right selection
this verse gives direction
just heed to its suggestion

a morning bowl of oats
and such other like type grains
provides one with the oomph
for a colon cleansing drain

add such an herbal mix
of some fresh crisp leafy greens
and their trusted sidekick
those bountiful healthful beans

top with some lovely fruit
carrots and similar roots
the inside garbage and smoot

gets the botanical boot
junk moved out of the way
with veggies tasty when ripe
water four pounds a day
clear out the internal pipes

I beg you remember this
to achieve body fitness
take in this verbose gist
of a fiber optimist

FREE DAY AT THE EXPO

By Lindsay Lake

Today could be considered a miracle, especially for Chicago in 2019. Twenty eight degrees, socked in cloud cover, pitch black night. The tops of the skyscrapers went missing in a winter gray out. No wind. Had there been a wind there would not have been a line all the way down to the Prudential building for the Warhol exhibition. Last five days!

Each person in line looks like they can pay to get in. I can. I came on a free day as an act of desperation. Something big to do to get my mind out of my mind.

The two kids in front of me are not dressed for the weather. Neither am I, for that matter, but I don't care if I'm cold. The boy in front of me wears a lightweight hoodie and Under Armour pants. He slides both hands down the front of them. His tiny girlfriend noticed.

"Get your hands out of there," she said, grabbing at his elbows. "It looks funny."

"I don't care. I'm freezing."

A tall lady in front of them turns around. "Damn… and I have a big winter coat in the trunk of my car. I just thought of that," she said to the kids. "Damn it's cold."

"How long is it?" the tiny girl asked.

"About down to here." The tall lady points below her knees.

"No… I mean how far away. We'll hold your place in line," the girl said.

"Sure ... we can do that," the boy agreed, bouncing from one foot to another.

The kids have big eager eyes. Like they are happy an adult talked to them like an adult.

"My car is just down the street ... It's really not that cold," the tall lady said, pulling the thin hood of her cotton jacket over her head.

The line moves. All at once. About ten feet.

Across from the front door a man sits on a crate beating a plastic bucket with drumsticks. Somehow the beat keeps me warm. I don't know what that's about. How can a drumbeat keep you warm? I think this over scientifically.

Beside him sits another frail looking man on another crate. He smiles a big smile displaying poor dental care. He glances frequently at a bundle by his feet.

"Is that a cat?" the tiny girl asks.

"Is that a real cat?" She turns to her boyfriend. "That cat has to be freezing." She thinks it over.

"Why would someone bring their cat?" She talks to herself.

"That coat is huge." The tall lady said to the shivering teenagers. "It's big ... and blue... and filled with down. It has a big hood with fur all over. We could wrap up in it like a tent."

She pantomimes the description of the coat. All three of them laugh out loud imagining themselves huddled underneath the tall women's coat.

The line moves.

Heads bob out of the line straining to make out if the object on the ground in front of the frail man is a real live cat.

"That is a cat. That's a real cat. It has on a jacket," the tiny girl with the best vision said.

"That cat looks warmer than we are," the tall lady said to the college aged girl in front of her.

The college girl humped a huge backpack, and a scarf round around her neck so many times it looked like a blanket.

"I can't believe this line," the college girl said. "I was here the other day and I walked right in."

"Free day?" the tall lady said.

"Oh, free day. Sure. Well ... I'm staying. I have to go back to school and I really want to see it again ... it's that good."

The tall lady and the college girl talk on, and walk side-by-side like instant friends.

The line moves.

The tall lady glances at her cell phone. One hour till closing time.

Two identical girls in front of the student talk to each other displaying their identical profiles.

104

The line moves.

They start up the steps.

I count the steps.

"We're running out of time," one twin said.

"I'm gonna stick it out. There's so much to see," her friend replied.

The line moves.

I am close enough to clearly see a sleeping live cat at the foot of the friendly man with bad teeth. Plus a sign by the cat.

CAT LIVES MATTER

People drop money into a jar by the sign.

"Do you see this?" the tall lady said to the student. "This guy knows America doesn't give two cents about humans ... but mess with their pets - "

"I know," the student said. "Pet insurance."

"Yeah... Pet hospitalization insurance."

They both shake their heads.

The tall lady glances up at the banners of the museum and back down at the cat. "I don't understand anything anymore," she says.

They make it up the stairs and into the outer door.

One of the twins knocks the door shut blocking any warmth from floating out of the museum to the masses. The student props the door open again. It shut again, and a third time.

"What's going on?" the twin said to the twin.

The student whispered to her.

"The person in front of you is bumping it."

"I should've been able to figure that out. Thank you."

The student looks proud of herself. Established as the leader of the group, she turns to the shivering teenagers.

"Come up here you two. You're freezing," she said and the kids move into the warm air.

Inside the door the group is greeted by a woman even taller than the tall lady. She explains the Warhol exhibit is full. They are about to cut off ticket sales, and unfortunately, but surely, we would not be able to get a ticket.

"I don't know," said the tiny teenager to her boyfriend. "Should we take a chance? I don't even know who Warhol is."

"You know… the Campbell Soup can," the tall lady said.

"Oh sure."

They pack into the queue.

The museum staffer gave her spiel to each person individually.

"You're not going to say what I think you're going to say," I say. She did. "I'll stay in line since we're all friends now," I say.

The queue gets tighter. More packed in. More claustrophobic. I start to heat up. Without the kids, the student, the twins or the tall lady in front of me noticing, I push my way out the back of the line.

I swing by the museum gift shop packed full of Warhol merch. A real brand. Mao on a mug. Marilyn stationary. An Elvis tote bag. And the crème de la crème a $190.00 Warhol self-portrait silk scarf. Suddenly, as clear as a new day, I can see that silk scarf wrapped around that cat out front like the college girls fashion scarf. I wonder if I even want to see the exhibit.

Outside the line is gone. The drummer is gone. The cat is gone. It feels good to be in the fresh air. It feels good to be alone on the cold dark streets of Chicago. It feels good to stretch my legs stiff from standing.

I look off in the distance and head that way.

GOD WALKS INTO A BAR...

By Tom Hernandez

Just so we're clear: I am God.

Yes, *that* God. Well, the *only* God, if you want to be technical, although at one time many years ago there were several other so-called "gods" who got a lot of attention from various prophets and spiritual leaders of all kinds, but trust Me on this, there is only one, and I AM...Who AM.

Ha! You see what I did there? No pronouns, no gender. That tends to throw you a bit, but it is what it is, and I am what I AM. Anyway, I am introducing myself right from the start so that there's no question, no doubt, and worst of all, no nit-picking from the literary types who may be reading this as to why the narrator in this story knows what everyone is thinking.

Which is kind of a neat twist, since so many of My Creation have dared to think that they knew what *I* was thinking. Ha! My thoughts are so much bigger than your ability to comprehend. It's really kind of silly for you to even try. I kept telling you that for a long time and some of you got it, but then you got into the Faith business and you had to have something to sell to the masses. I get it, really, I do. I don't like it...but that's for another conversation.

Sorry! I got sidetracked there a bit. Fair warning, I sometimes do that. I don't talk directly to My Creation very often, no matter what those Fundamentalists think. It's too hard. I can't ever get a word in edgewise...so when I do have a chance to talk, I sometimes overshare...

So, as you may have heard, I like to visit My Creation every now and then just to check things out, chat a bit, hear what you have to say. You'd think social media would have made that easier, since everyone can share their every thought about everything all the time. About that, I'll just say this: just because you can do something doesn't mean you should. And contrary to popular belief, social media is not Satan's handiwork. Not because he couldn't. He's very clever. I know from first-hand experience.

Rather, he's just not that evil. I mean, come on…to create something that feeds humanity's most base, arrogant, self-centered instincts and make it as close as a few easy clicks on a computer with no awareness much less regard for the possible consequences? Only Man would do that. Still, Old Goat Face sure appreciates it. And yes, he does have accounts on all the biggies: Facebook, Twitter, Instagram. Of course, Snapchat is his favorite.

Darn it, I got sidetracked again. See what I mean?

So, to the point: I stopped at a local bar recently and sat down next to a patron. It doesn't really matter who it was. You're all the same to Me. Besides, this is just a random sampling, not a scientific process (and yes, I love science. Who do you think invented science? Although Satan had a hoof, er, I mean, a hand in trigonometry…)

But, for the sake of this story, let's just say it was an English-speaking American male, and I spoke to him as a Christian, since that's the faith system *he* was most familiar with. Really though, it could be any faith and any religion. Frankly, they're all the same, and they all end with Me, no matter what you call Me, or how you try to talk to Me. I've never understood why My Creation has never understood that. It's not a great mystery. I mean, *I* understand, of course! There's political power in division that unity simply doesn't offer. What I mean is, I don't understand why *you* don't understand. That kind of power creates more trouble than it's worth. But again, I digress…

Anyway, I introduced myself. And, My Creation doubted Me. No surprise. All that chitter-chatter about faith and trust usually goes right out the door when someone sits down next to you claiming to be Me. It happens a lot, actually. Suffice it to say, I knew what was coming.

"So, you're God, eh?" he said. He peered at the mirror behind the bar. He was trying to see if My reflection was there next to his own between the bottles of hard liquor. It was.

"Hey, cut that out! I'm not a vampire," I said, startling him. His eyes snapped sheepishly back to mine, embarrassed at having been caught.

"Ok, well if you're God, then prove it."

"Oh, that's not a good start," I said. "Didn't you pay any attention in Sunday School? The Egyptians and the Red Sea? The ten commandments and the golden calf? Forty years walking in circles in the desert? The ending of 'Lost'? Testing Me usually doesn't end well."

"OK, let's just say you're God."

"I AM."

"Then what's your name?"

"I just told you. I AM. I knew what you were thinking and answered your question before you could even ask it. Because I'm you know, *I'm God.*"

"Fine, Mister I AM."

"Not Mister."

"Missus? You mean, like Mother Nature?"

"Nope, not Missus either. Just, I AM."

Uncertainty clouded his eyes, but he still played along. I have to say I appreciate honest pragmatism in My Creation. It helps weed out the real weirdos. People who believe everything will believe anything. Always dangerous.

"Ok, well then, can I buy you a drink?" he offered.

"Certainly."

"Really? I thought drinking was a sin."

"Not at all. What you do *after* you drink is sometimes sinful but drinking itself is fine. I want My Creation to enjoy the life I've given you – in moderation, of course! I love a good drink every now and again. Especially at weddings."

"Great. What'll it be?"

I looked him square in the eye. "Truthfully, I like all fermented beverages, but wine is my favorite. Are you *sure* you've heard about Me?"

He ordered a glass of a decent Merlot for Me, and another swill beer for himself. Yes, it is true, some beers and wines are better than others, and this was one of the cheapest and thinnest around. The kind you drink to get drunk, rather than to enjoy My handiwork. Ugh! But he was buying so what could I say?

He wound up to ask another question. "Now, please don't get angry. I don't want any floods. I left my ark at home!"

"Good one!" Honestly, it was not a particularly clever retort, but I try to ease My Creation's heart in many ways. Laughter is one of the best. In cases like this a little white lie doesn't hurt anything.

"I don't mean to test you or make you mad, but if you're *God*, like you say…" – he leaned over his drink and nudged Me in the ribs with his elbow and winked – "…then what was the greatest thing you ever gave us?"

"What *is* the greatest thing I ever gave My Creation. Not was. *Is*. The greatest thing I ever gave you is the gift that keeps on giving, as you like to say."

"Ah! Mister Tricky with the Words!"

"To answer your question, the greatest gift I ever gave My Creation is…"

"Wait, I know this one: Your son, Jesus."

"Yes."

"Ha! Score one for the doubting human!" He nodded his triumph.

"And no."

"What?" His eyes spun with puzzlement. Or maybe it was the booze.

"You see, Jesus was indeed my son, and he did indeed embody my love and grace better than any of you, but you're all my children, same as he was. You all have the exact same abilities, the same skills, the same resources as he did. The only difference was, he listened better."

I paused to let that golden nugget settle in his mental prospecting pan.

"No, my greatest gift to all of you was something simpler, yet infinitely more difficult: Freedom."

"Come again?"

"Freedom. Free will. The ability to choose. To determine what you will do. How you will treat others. Who you will love. Where and when – and even if – you will come home to Me. It's what puts you atop the rest of My Creation."

I sipped my wine, letting it roll around my tongue. Delicious! Grapes are truly one of My most inspired inventions.

"Well, that and opposable thumbs," I added. Another sip, swirl and swallow.

"And I'd also throw self-awareness in there, though most of you are so self-absorbed that it's impossible to be aware of anything, most especially yourselves."

He downed his beer and placed the empty mug on the bar. He paused. "Huh…that's pretty deep."

"Well, I am *God*. 'Deep' is kind of my thing."

"Ok, supposing you are actually who you say you are…"

"I AM."

"Right, right, that again. Supposing you are who you say you am…er, I mean, who you are…oh man, now you've got me all twisted up!" He took a deep breath, then tried again. "What I am trying to say is, I suppose then we've really fucked things up – oops, forgive my language!"

"Don't worry about it! Remember, I invented all words, not just *The Word*." Not a bad pun, if I do say so myself – and I've made a lot of them through the millennia. I offered a toothy grin.

"Hardy har, har…very funny."

His brain struggled to gather itself. I'd really put a lot on his mental plate, and it showed, but that's not my fault. Very few of you use more than a fraction of the intellect I gave you.

"So, you're saying we're responsible for just about every bad thing in our lives because of the choices we make?"

"Just about."

"War?"

"Yep."

"Starvation?"

"Uh-huh."

"The Holocaust."

"That was a bad one."

"Trump?"

"You even have to ask?"

"What about pain and disease?"

"Most of those are just a part of life. Your body is a glorious machine. All machines break. But yes, sometimes they break sooner or more often because of how you treat them."

His mouth hung agape. I gently pushed his chin up until his lips met. Finally, he spoke. "If you're the parent of everyone as you say, then you must be pretty mad at us."

"I have to be honest, you know, being God and all. It's been pretty disappointing."

The weight of a thousand simultaneous guilty thoughts dragged his gaze down to his hands.

"But there have been a few encouraging exceptions. Joan of Arc, Ghandi, Mother Teresa, Abraham Lincoln, that little girl who stood up to the Taliban even after they shot her in the head."

He smiled, relieved.

"And I have to say, Ringo Starr."

"Ringo? *Ringo* is your favorite Beatle?"

"Without question. I love his whole 'Peace and Love' thing. Comes straight from his heart. He really seems to get it."

"Wow! So, then, why in the world would you stick with us? Why haven't you – what's the word? Smite? – Why didn't you smite us all a long time ago?"

"For the same reason your parents didn't 'smite' you when they learned that you crashed the car when you went on a joy ride with your girlfriend while they were gone on vacation."

His brow crinkled.

"How did you know about…"

I stared at him as hard as I could.

"Oh, that's right…God."

"And the answer is, because I know I raised you better, and I have faith that you will eventually do the right thing. Which, by the way, is my favorite Spike Lee movie."

A hesitant smile peeked from his eyes. "Really? After everything we've done?"

"Of course. I know in my heart that you'll get there eventually. Listen: there's a lot of hooey in your holy books. But you know the part about me making you in my image?"

He nodded.

"That part is absolutely true. And listen, the fact of the matter is, I've made mistakes myself."

"Really?" He laughed a little. "God has made mistakes?"

"Of course. Have you seen the platypus? I could never quite get that one right. The point is, I believe in you, even if you don't believe in Me."

Clearly my message hit him like a ton of bricks. Or he'd finally had too much to drink. Either way, he shook his head. Confusion skittered across his brain like water bugs on a pond. He didn't speak for several minutes, not knowing what quite to say. Finally, he broke the silence.

"Hey, do you want another glass of wine?"

"That's very kind. Thank you."

As he waved at the bartender, I reached over to the water bottle sitting at the edge of the bar. I held my hand over the top and...well, *you know*. He turned back, looked at the bottle, then my glass, then at Me.

"Really?" he said. "You couldn't just wait for me to order you another glass?"

"Well I could have, but why waste good water?" I smiled.

I poured a glass of the most magnificent Cabernet Sauvignon. Deep purple. Lush, dark berry flavors. Bold and complex finish, not too heavy on the palette.

Dare I say it was heavenly.

IF I DIE BEFORE I WAKE

By Tom Hernandez

I opened my eyes.

Darkness. Had it happened?

No, the fire in my gut and pounding behind my eyes from another restless night confirmed I was still alive. Then, "Good morning, Dad. Time to wake up." My daughter's voice was always a welcome treat, and today, even more so.

She threw open the shades. Late-winter sunshine poured through the window, so sharp the dust magically materialized in the air like specks on an X-ray. I squeezed my eyelids tighter to block the light. No luck.

"How'd you sleep?" she chirped.

"Honey, I haven't slept in days." The lack of rest clouded my sight. I instinctively rubbed my eyes, hoping they'd clear.

"Oh, come on." She cheerfully tugged at the blankets tucked around my chin. "I have your breakfast going downstairs. Eat a little something and you'll feel better."

"I doubt it."

"Why?"

"Because today's the day."

"What's so special about today?" Jenny flowed around the room like a spring breeze, my twenty-eight-year-old angel picking my clothes from the floor, straightening the blankets at my feet, fluffing the pillows behind my head. Maybe – probably? – for the last time.

"You know very well."

"I have no idea what you're talking about."

"I'm going to die today."

Jenny slammed to a halt. Her head snapped around. Her eyes, mirroring her smiling demeanor only a few seconds ago now lasered her anger. "Stop saying that, Dad, that's not true and you know it."

"But it is true. That's what that idiot doctor told me. He said, 'A year, maybe more.'"

114

"Right," Jenny said. "A year, *maybe more.*"

"I'm sorry honey, I appreciate your optimism, but I'm pretty sure what he said was, '*A year*, maybe more.' Today is one year since he pronounced my death sentence, so…"

Jenny sat at the end of the bed. "OK, fine, if you insist on being like this, then please let me know when you're going to expire so I can plan the rest of my day. I have other things to do than to sit around here waiting to hear your death rattle."

Her flat stare was deadpanned proof of her wit, dry as a dinosaur bone in the desert. Jenny's sense of humor was a welcome gift from her mother, and a reminder of the only other woman I ever loved. Still, it stung sometimes. "Ouch! That hurts. Your mother, rest her soul, would have never talked to a dying man that way."

Jenny's head drooped under the weight of a smile. "Oh yes she would've. If she'd lived, she would have threatened to kill you herself for talking like this."

She laughed, and I smiled too, then took her left hand. My thumb gently caressed her beautiful ring signifying her marriage to a wonderful young man who loved her very much. Not as much as me, but enough to understand when she started spending a night, then two, now three or four a week babysitting me as this goddamned disease stole my life one minute at a time. Which is to say, enough to earn a father's respect and appreciation. It had been bad enough losing my darling wife to her own illness just as I was diagnosed.

"You sure are one special kid," I said, choking on the whispered words, struggling against a wave of tears.

"I'm not a kid, Daddy. I'm a big girl." She smiled easily. Our secret code for the inside joke she'd been making to me since she was six. Memories of her childhood brightly colored by her independent spirit and piss-and-vinegar attitude filled the corners of my mind. "I know honey. I know. I know." Suddenly, I felt tired. "Do you mind if I rest a bit now?"

Jenny stood and headed toward the bedroom door. "Only if you promise not to die before I come back."

"I'll do my best, but I can't promise anything."

"Ugh! Daddy…"

I don't know how long I dozed. It felt like a few hours, but it couldn't have been more than the few minutes Jenny needed to whip up a light breakfast. She set the tray on the dresser and approached the head of the bed.

She gently lifted me under my arms to position me higher on the stack of pillows behind my head. "I brought some green tea, some scrambled eggs and a piece of plain toast. Nothing too heavy. Don't want to go against your medicine and upset your stomach."

She turned back to the dresser to get the tray. I waved her off. "Thank you honey, but really, I'm not hungry."

"Why not? Are you sick?"

"Well, I'm going to be dead soon, if that's what you mean."

"Daddy, stop that, please," Jenny said. "It really upsets me when you talk that way. And no, that's not what I mean."

"Alright, I'm sorry. My stomach is fine." I tapped on my forehead. "I have a lot on my mind is all, with it being my last…" I caught myself and sheepishly avoided Jenny's glare.

She circled the bed and laid next to me, propped on her elbow so I didn't have to turn too much. Always thoughtful, this one, even down to the end.

"OK," Jenny said, "for the sake of argument, let's say that today is your very last day on this earth. What is so heavy on your mind that you won't eat the gourmet breakfast I made?"

How does one answer such an immense, intimate question? Especially to a person – the only person -- one holds above all others? Carefully, I decided. Delicately, but honestly.

"My sins. My many, many sins."

Jenny rolled her eyes.

"All right, I'll bite. What *enormous sins* have you committed?" she teased.

"Jennifer Ann, I'm serious." I paused. "I have done some terrible things in my life. Things I am embarrassed about. Ashamed of. Things I feel terrible for doing to you, your mother, lots of people."

"Wow. Except for when I got in trouble as a kid, the only time you've ever used my full name is when you told me Mom had died." She sat up and turned again now to face me head-on, her

116

arms wrapped around her raised knees. "Sins like what? You didn't kill anyone, did you?"

"No, of course not."

"Steal anything?"

"Nothing big."

"Cheat on Mom?"

I took a breath, exhaled, then took another. "Let's just say, once or twice some innocent flirting went a few steps past 'innocent.' But your mother knew about all of it -- and held me accountable."

Jenny gazed at me, then dropped her eyes. She traced one of the flowers on the bedspread with her finger for a few seconds. "Well, I guess there's not much to say about that now that Mom is gone. In the big picture, I suppose that's not such a terrible thing…"

I quickly cut her off. "But that's not the worst of it. That's not what's bothering me." Now it was my turn to look away from her. My beautiful, smart, intuitive girl. Her sharp, blue eyes that could soothe one second and cut to the bone the next contracted with exasperation.

"Alright, I give up! What's the big sin, Dad?"

"You know, I'm not the religious type…"

"I know, my wedding was one of the only times I've ever seen you in church."

"…Right. So, I don't say this lightly, but I think I've cut my ties with God…or Mother Nature...or the universe...or heaven…whatever you call it."

"Darn it, Dad, spit it out!"

"I don't know…" The ideas that had overtaken my mind the last few weeks now struggled to take shape. "This is just hard for me to put into words. I guess, for lack of any better explanation, I've come to realize just how disconnected I am from other people."

Jenny expelled a loud sigh of relief. "Is that all? I thought you had done something really bad."

"But it *is* bad, honey. I've spent years pushing people away, creating some stupid myth of mystery. I wasted my entire life building walls when I could've – should've – been building bridges with all the people in my life. And for what? To protect my privacy."

Jenny's eyes crinkled and she laughed. "I'm confused. Your job put you in the public eye a lot. I remember people interrupting you all the time, wanting autographs or pictures, at dinner, the movies, ball games," she said. "I'm just your daughter, so what do I know? But it seems to me like you had good reason to want a little space."

I'm sure it was the medicine confusing my memory, but for a moment I swore her mother stared back at me. So trusting. So kind. So forgiving.

"Of course, I had a reason. But it's the worst possible one: I just didn't want to be bothered. True, I don't like many people. Most everyone I ever met was thoughtless, self-centered, mean, stupid. But honestly, it was just my own arrogance. My ego was so big, there was no room for anyone else. I created a mountain of bullshit of the highest order. Turns out I was the stupid, petty, small one."

My hands trembled weakly as I took hers again. "I never wanted anyone near me. I didn't want to be responsible for another life. Now that I want someone, need someone, there's no one. I feel so stupid, so…" I dropped my eyes, ashamed of my horrible truth, then raised them again. "I don't mind being alone, Jenny. But *being lonely* is a terrible thing."

A tear wet Jenny's cheek. "Daddy, I'm so sorry! If I had known I would have come over more, done more!"

"No, no, my love bug! You haven't done anything wrong. I didn't mean it that way. Goodness, you're the only person I have left. I am *so* grateful you listen to me at all. No, it's all my own fault."

My voice caught in my throat as pain knifed through my gut and sucked the air from my lungs. My grip on Jenny's hands tightened, then released as the ache in my belly ebbed. I breathed a few times to regain my strength, but the new words seemed heavier than usual, draining what little energy I had only a second ago.

"I finally understand what everyone means when they talk about heaven being the shared space between people," I croaked

118

weakly. "That's the good news. The bad news is, I realize now that I've thrown away the greatest gift God ever gave -- the love and friendship of others. And now that it's too late for me to do anything about it, I'm terrified God will punish me."

"Punish you how?" Jenny's soft voice matched her gentle, but firm grip.

"By forcing me to maintain the distance I created. By keeping me away from all the people who cared about me." I paused, trying to stave off the army of tears I'd been fighting for days.

"By not letting me near the one person who I ever let get close to me. The one person who understood me. Accepted me. Forgave me." I took a deep breath, held it, then exhaled.
"I am terrified God will never let me see your mother again."

At long last the tears came. I couldn't help it. These thoughts had consumed nearly every waking moment the last few days. To hear them out loud from my own mouth somehow made them even more horrible. I felt like Frankenstein that awful moment his monster rose from the table charged with the life he'd given it.

"Oh, Daddy, don't be silly. God isn't cruel."

"Oh Jenny, *now* who's being silly? Have you *actually read* the Bible? How about today's newspaper? Look around us, Jenny. If God's not cruel, He's at least got a wicked sense of humor."

She took a deep breath, eased her legs over the edge of the bed and slowly, wordlessly stood. She lifted me, fluffed the pillows and lowered me back, then gently kissed my forehead. Like I'd done to her a million times when she was a child. I was grateful for her silence. My swollen throat wouldn't have allowed a word to pass if she'd said anything.

A minute passed, maybe two. Then, "Dad, for your sake, for all our sakes, I hope and pray and trust and believe with every part of my being that you are wrong," she said, offering the gentlest, subtlest reprimand I think I've ever gotten.

She tucked the blankets around me and opened the window. A soft afternoon breeze, warm enough to suggest spring was just around the corner, danced lightly into the room.

"I believe God forgives our sins, even – especially – if we don't forgive them ourselves. And that includes the sin of refusing His gifts."

Jenny lifted the food tray from the dresser and turned to go, but then set it back down. She returned to the bedside, gently nudged me over, took my left hand, and sat.

"Most of all, I believe God even forgives us for forsaking Him. Or Mother Nature. Or the universe. Whatever you call it."

She smiled and winked at me. One more joke for the road, I guess.

"Otherwise, how would we possibly survive the unthinkable evil that we create? The walls we build between and around each other? The hatred that ignores and belittles God's love? All the god-forsaken things we do to God's own creation in God's name?" Jenny said. "For me, a loving, forgiving God is the only thing that makes any sense in a world that makes no sense at all."

Suddenly, the air seemed to shimmer with the glittering grace of her conviction. My chest swelled with equal parts sorrow and pride.

"My beautiful child, how did you get to be so wise?" My voice stumbled, heavy with sincere awe for this soul, at once child-like and mature beyond measure, who was the last and final bridge to whatever this world is, and the next world might be.

"I listened to the people around me. Friends. Family. You. Mom," she said. "Then I listened to my heart."

Her words were so beautiful and encouraging. Yet, reality gave me little hope, and even less comfort. "That's all wonderful, and I am glad for you, but I don't have time now to fix all my mistakes."

"Sure, you do. There's always tomorrow." Jenny bent and kissed my cheek

"But what if there's no tomorr--"

"There's *always* tomorrow, Daddy." She frowned, giving no ground.

We volleyed for a while longer about the nature of Nature, spirituality, what might come next -- whether "next" would be in this room, or somewhere else -- and what that might look like wherever or whatever or whenever it came.

We discussed philosophy, religion, politics. We eventually turned to less contentious subjects: memories of her childhood and comparisons of her own young marriage to her mother's and my early years as a couple. I dozed between debate points, waking to my snores only to find her waiting patiently for me to answer. My admiration for my daughter–and regret for my imminent passing-- grew with each bright, intuitive, thoughtful, sharp, funny idea and statement that she spoke.

Finally, the emotional burden of the day weighed heavy on my heart and tugged at my eyelids. The breakfast tray remained untouched on the dresser, as the afternoon sun faded.

"Honey, I'd talk to you forever, if I could. But I'm tired. I think I might really sleep more than a few minutes this time." My thin laugh sounded more like a whisper than a chuckle. "Do you mind if I take a nap?"

"Of course not! Now close your eyes," she ordered. "Don't think too much. Just rest. You've had a hard day. I'll wake you when it's time for dinner." She clicked the light switch and pulled the door behind her, leaving it open enough so I could see the light in the hallway.

I lay still, staring into the semi-darkness, afraid I'd once again find myself in the crossfire between the rest I so desperately sought, and the flashing explosions of anxiety that had kept sleep at bay for days.

Jenny's words rolled through my brain. I thought about her faith in ultimate goodness. Her understanding of the mysteries of love. Her forgiveness of human failing.

My body pointlessly protested the pain building inside with every shallow breath, one relentless brick after another. Yet I felt a new calm. A strange, but welcome sense of peace. I turned toward the glow outside the bedroom door.

Then I closed my eyes.

LIVING ON THE EDGE

By Denise M. Baran-Unland

Enjoy an excerpt from the third book in the BryonySeries young adult vampire trilogy "Staked!"
For the full book description, visit bryonyseries.com.

The sun set low in the orange-gold and black sky, while the evening wind commenced its wispy lullaby. The boughs and wildflowers bent and swayed, even as the shivering littlest pixies scurried to their respective abodes, where they would bundle into tufts of cotton and toast their diminutive toes before matchstick bonfires.

Initial audience departed, Glorna ceased his reel and cocked his head to listen to the first alluring notes of the evening wind, always a delightful surprise, whether they crooned a fluttering breeze or blasted an occasional fortissimo gale.

Assured he could reproduce tonight's song, Glorna coiled his toes around the old, gnarled branches; rested his head against the broad, lobed leaves; raised his pointed face to the moon; and scattered his musical strains across the heavens. Each piping perfectly complemented the whistle blowing through his oak, and he contentedly sighed and merged with the ethereal music.

While he played, the filmy, cornflower-blue fairies flitted about the evening primroses and moonflowers. They pried open the delicate blooms and released into the night air the hundreds of supernatural beings that dwelled within them. Soon, the ground sylphs emerged, their transparent, mauve wings glowing under the full moonlight. Even the gray water sprites hovering over Quixotic Pond, paused their patrol to bask in the haunting tune.

It was a perfect life, and he was grateful for the steward's generous gift of consciousness. One moment he did not exist, and the next he sat cross-legged under a toadstool, the tips of his pointed ears grazing its velvety, cone-shaped cap as he blew a treble jig. When he willed it, Glorna expanded to the height of a full-grown man, one that kept an immaculate cottage and bountiful garden. Other times, he shrank smaller than a butterfly, scaled trees with the agility of a lizard, and glided through the air with the easy speed of a dragonfly.

With his profound musical abilities and passion for song and dance, he should have happily dwelled in the mounds with the other trooping fairies, their home ever since the Milesians defeated the Tuatha de Danaan. However, his mischievous tendencies, high intelligence, and preference for toiling alone set him apart from that group and turned the poor steward's hair white with worry over how and where to classify this atypical sprite, as he didn't neatly fit any category in the steward's entire kingdom.

He certainly could have made a fine leprechaun, for his solitary nature suited it, if only his penchant was shoemaking, not music. He enjoyed mischief, but that alone was too shallow for him, so becoming a fear dearg or pooka was unthinkable. He abhorred strong drink, so joining the cluricahns was impossible. He was too full of life to enjoy an existence as a dullahan, but his marked preference for human traits prohibited roanism. However, this fairy had a fierce, protective spirit, which made the steward seriously consider deeming him a dinnshenchas, although he worried about Glorna's scornful tendencies. He finally deemed the fairy a wood sprite, and, with the first challenge settled, the steward began the search for a proper vocation.

The rebellion began with his name. The steward called him Lugh because of the enchanting effect his melodic whistling had on human and sidhe alike. It provoked euphoria during times of feasting and frolicking, released poignant emotion during moments of sadness, comforted under affliction, and eliminated insomnia by inducing a deliciously, soporific state.

It was the steward's right to name him, and no one disputed it. But the strong winds during a particularly heavy rainfall so badly whipped the branches of the oaks that its limbs scratched his windowpane, as they begged him for relief: "Glorna! Glorna!" The fairy decided that sacred trees were wiser than a nonexistent steward and adopted the name, which generated his first censure by verse:

The wood sprite tied to his pride
Should heed the one guarding his hide
When he nurtured the gall

To make his own call
Something great inside of him died.

Perhaps the steward was right, because after the first offense, Glorna's sense of propriety became greatly reduced, and more daring infractions followed: conversing with mortals in their sleep, tripping anyone who stepped on a fairy mound, tossing acorns onto mortals' paths, and risking real exposure by leaving tracks of dancing footprints in botanical gardens. With each offense, the steward increased Glorna's verbal chastisement, which only caused Glorna to laugh with glee and scamper away to the next escapade.

Nearing despair, the steward changed tactics. He summoned Glorna to his chamber and slyly praised Glorna's superlative talents as an independent fairy. Instead of punishment, the steward offered him a reward, the position of protecting a very old oak tree in southwest France, a tree older than the steward himself. Duties included consuming the grubs and fungus threatening to destroy it and nipping any axes poised to chop it down. In the evenings, Glorna would be free to make his music. The bargain was struck, the first Glorna would make with the desperate steward.

The initial few centuries were glorious ones, for Glorna was free to live as he pleased, answering to no one, for he was far from the steward's controlling grasp. The feeling was mutual, for the steward no longer endured complaints from the other fairies about this mutinous fabrication of his mind, leaving him free to rule with the ruthlessness he so esteemed. Glorna's voracious appetite soon eliminated any pestilence lurking on the tree, and his sharp, little teeth cut deeply into the arms of all axmen who approached it, frightening them into abandoning their tools and fleeing for safety miles away from Glorna's tree. Then came the attacker that changed the direction of the story.

Looking back, Glorna wasn't certain if this particular lumberjack was not easily daunted, or if Glorna merely had tired of dining on insects and molds, because, this time, he drew blood. Glorna had eaten meat once at Clancy's house and enjoyed it, but the sting of red flesh straight from its source enflamed him, and, for a moment, he felt one with the dearg-due who rose at night to drink the blood of past lovers. Glorna hesitated no longer. With siphon-like power, the fairy drained every drop.

If only his action hadn't made the news! That particular tree, his beloved tree, was slated for destruction to make room for a highway. A national movement began to save the enchanted tree, which now attracted thousands of tourists. Reports of French vampire oak trees circulated past reality and into the deluded realm of the steward. With wringing hands, the steward sought out Glorna and demanded the reason for this audacity. Glorna defended his actions, for wasn't he sent to protect the tree? The steward worried that once a sprite tasted blood, he might frantically seek more, jeopardizing the entire sidhe race, something the steward could not allow. Glorna minimized the steward's alarm, but a growing frenzy for more blood now consumed him, and he wondered how long he could repress it. This new thirst scared him, even as it excited him, and he wondered if blood gulped by night tasted as good as blood quaffed by day. The fearsome light in the steward's eyes told him that an eternal, rhyming punishment awaited him, even if he curbed his lust, for what might the other fairies attempt if they knew what Glorna had accomplished with no penalty? Luckily for him, the all-wise, all-knowing, and all-powerful steward had a wonderful solution.

Every fairy knows that consistent breeding weakens its bloodline, consequently producing hideously malformed offspring, which can only be strengthened once again with the fairest of human blood. Yet, trying to stop a fairy from breeding, especially during nights of feasting and frolicking, is like trying to stop night from following day. Co-mingling humans with the leprechauns is the optimal solution, but enticing real people to the job is nearly impossible. Historically, fairies swapped their unwanted infants for human ones, raised them as their own, and appropriately betrothed them in due time. Occasionally, when these fairy children expired at a rate quicker than their parents could reproduce them, carefully selected pieces of wood were magically quickened and charged with the duty of imitating their human counterparts. Furious with the steward for the lack of respect for his tree and eager to explore new lands, Glorna accepted the title of "changeling." With eyes of wonder, Glorna examined the oak piano leg that would soon become a new "him."

The glow was short-lived. The steward hailed a woodsman, indicated Glorna's tree, and ordered its immediate death, as punishment for the fairy's murderous deed. An anguished Glorna vigorously protested, but the steward heartlessly laughed, wound a spool of thread around the fairy, as neatly as any seamstress might, and tucked him into his kilt for the journey back to the underworld, a journey that could be hard or easy, long or quick, depending on the steward's present mood, for he controlled all elements of the story.

These circumstances abruptly changed, for Glorna, still raging and vowing to avenge his noble tree, was suddenly inside the ramshackle cottage of Eircheard, the steward's head shoemaker and aspiring woodworker. Eircheard, while not exactly compassionate, pitied the trapped sprite, unrolled him from his threaded prison, and fed him a slice of his famed Irish soda bread.

As Glorna munched the wonderfully tangy food, as flavorful as any grub he'd ever eaten, Eircheard carefully took measurements for Glorna's human outer wrap, leaving sufficient space for the computer chip brain. The steward watched each step with eyes hungry for power and control, but Eircheard foiled them both. He, respectfully, of course, informed the steward that he worked better unsupervised. In the meantime, didn't the steward have ruthless business somewhere in time to conduct?

With a promise to return by the morrow and threats of rhyming reprimands if the task was not complete, the steward exited the cottage by way of the front door, an amazing occurrence for Glorna, since he was accustomed to seeing the steward blend into air. After pouring a large draught into a tin mug, draining it, pouring another, and then shoving a stout clay pipe between his teeth, Eircheard grabbed Glorna and the rest of his home brew and then stepped outside to the clearing in front of his hut. Dark, thick woods surrounded Eircheard's property on all sides, lit only by the unprotected, crackling fire several yards from his door.

Eircheard set his mug near the fire and settled himself on the wide, old log before it. A collection of tools and the scuffed piano leg lay close by. Glorna, really curious now, speculated how the tipsy dwarf might create a new being from this odd assortment of implements and materials. With a chuckle, Eircheard stuffed Glorna into his shirt pocket, but Glorna's fingers grabbed the edge and pulled himself up to observe the process. He didn't have long to wait, for Eircheard picked up his hand drill and the piano leg. Balancing the misshapen wood between his stubby legs, Eircheard bored a hole three-quarters into the wood and then dropped Glorna into the abyss. Glorna opened his mouth to object, but wood chips sealed his prison shut. The actual carving now began. Bored, Glorna sank into sleep. When he awakened, he was lying inside a clear plastic bin in a completely new world.

LOOP

By S. Houk

If an owl
calls your name
can it mean
that you are mortal?
But you knew that.

It's a loop back.
It's a song I play a lot.
Not wanting to get it wrong.
I put it on "repeat".

LUNCH LESSONS

By James Moore

The junior high school lunch hour provides an anthropological
Mecca as a location with which to observe interactions between
people. The most impressive lunch time lesson that I received
about human relationships did not take place in the cafeteria.
Instead, it happened at a counselor's office.

Pizza Day

I met my childhood best friend, Richard while we were in
the sixth grade. We did not click right away. However, one spring
Saturday we ran into each other at the "Y," also known as the
Y.M.C.A. Thereafter, we hung out. We talked a lot usually about
music, girls, and our coveted "baddest" rankings where we
discussed who among us boys would win in a fight against another.
In addition, playing Saturday baseball games at the "Y" provided a
staple of our summers. Ah, the good ole days. But, I digress.

I was a brown bagger, one who brought my lunch with me
to school. Richard, however, ate the hot meals offered by the
school. Typically, lunch carrying kids would get to the tables first
because they did not wait in line. It was by sheer chance or on
occasion that we sat together at lunch. Pizza day was different. We
both ate the hot meal when pizza was served.

1 Lesson, 2 Lunches

The Lord used pizza to prove a point. I will expound. The
cafeteria resided on the first floor whereas the lockers were
stationed on the second and third floors. One fine day, Richard
found himself in a predicament. He had not taken his books to his
higher level locker as students started lining up. Ah, but he had a
friend. We just sauntered over to Mr. Schaefer's office. Richard
asked the friendly school counselor if he could keep his books in

129

the office. The school office pleasantly agreed and then we were off to lunch featuring the prized pizza.

Flash forward to a future pizza day. It was my turn to be late. In fact, I wasn't even initially late. I thought I'd be slick and do same thing Richard did and just ask nice Mr. Schaefer to keep my books in his office. He wasn't so nice to me. He was polite, didn't yell or anything, but he said no. Furthermore, he lectured me about how it was my responsibility to take my books to my locker bla bla bla. The speech lasted so long I barely made it to lunch on time. What was the difference between Richard and I?

Richard earned the trust of the school counselor. He proved himself dependable doing errands for the school official. He was consistent and displayed an attitude of gratitude. Me, I was some boy Mr.Schaefer didn't know from Adam. I was an unknown, unheard of somebody asking a favor of him. It's all about the value of relationship, Richard had it and I didn't.

New Lease on Life

Hezekiah, a good king of Judah, the Hebrew's southern nation, similarly had this kind of trust with the Lord. I am not saying that the Lord does favors by us because we deserve these. As the Word says salvation is by grace lest any man boast. However, God undoubtedly responds better to some than others.

Hezekiah in his old age was feeling it. He fell ill. One day the prophet Isaiah delivered a message to him from the Lord. He said, "Set thine house in order; for thou shalt die and not live." (2 Kings 20;1) Hezekiah was saddened by this. He wept as he prayed. He also reminded God of his well-established record as a faithful servant. I contend that God did not respond to the weeping so much as he did the record. Relationship matters. Hezekiah got his prayer through, Isaiah returned with good news announcing fifteen more years of life and to boot the Lord displayed a miracle as proof of his promise. (see 2 Kings 20:1-11)

Lest we forget, Hezekiah had something to talk about when he read his record. The Scriptures say that "he did that which was right in the sight of the Lord." (see 2 Kings 18:3) He rid the country of idol-like influences not the least of which was the brass serpent that hailed back to Moses day. He established himself. Apparently, he already knew the value of relationship before his new lease on life. I wonder if he learned this back when he was in the biblical era equivalent of junior high. Just saying.

NEMESIS

By Colleen H. Robbins

I have plied the seven seas and looked on barbarous coasts. I have fought the kraken to my last breath, and survived to tell the tale. But the darkness above has become my nemesis.

The first time the darkness drifted in, I nearly died. The great darkness spawned smaller patches of darkness, and those patches hid the aliens with their metal probes. The pain was near unbearable when the probes pierced my side.

I lost control, raging against the darkness. I smashed. I roared. Small, thin aliens struggled and died around me. I bit one in the leg.

The alien's leg came off in my mouth. Still raging, I tried to swallow. The leg slid halfway down, and stuck. I coughed, I squirmed, I threw myself into the darkness. My throat swelled entirely shut. My gut spasmed, and the leg flew from my mouth with the speed of the striking shark.

I approached the larger darkness, took a deep breath, and attacked. The darkness withdrew, but I did not stop until every smaller patch of darkness was gone.

The probe in my side hurts whenever I move too quickly.

I escaped that time, but now the darkness is back. As is the thin alien, leg regrown. Its face is covered in seal fur, and it covers one eye with a long tube. Did it expect to hide from me this way?

The alien, pale, but not as pale as I, stares at me from the edge of the darkness, long eye pointed in my direction. There is a cry, and another, and the long eye turns away.

I hear cries of distress. The aliens are chasing a large family group of my kind, including several young. No! They cannot! I charge when I see the probes come out.

The aliens surrounded us, sticking us with probes and capturing some of the larger females. We fight desperately, but it is no use. By the time the sun sinks below the horizon, it is over. Most do not live through the experience. Their bodies turn up in the rolling waves, torn by sharks.

We few who survive, scarred and in pain, we let our rage loose. The darkness is destroyed, vanishing beneath the waves. The aliens soon follow.

I feel another probe enter my side. A small group of aliens has crept up on me, my nemesis among them. I leap and crash against the water, trying to knock the probe loose. I roll to pull the strands from their hands.

Instead, I find myself caught in the trap of crossed strands that tighten on my body. My nemesis crosses the water and climbs up on my back, probe ready at hand. I roll again, trying to knock him off. His seal face leers as he catches a hand in the strands that wrap me.

The other aliens retreat as my nemesis, now caught in the strands himself, sinks down into the depths with me. I feel him move against my side, even after he is dead. I can never evade him again, but I survive. I am the white whale.

PARTY CRASHER

By Colleen H. Robbins

Darlene combed and sprayed her hair, then pulled the shoulder of her dress up to cover her prominent honeybee tattoo. "Save the bees," she muttered to herself, "for they will save you."

A bit of work around her eyes—liner, shadow, and mascara--and a lipstick tucked in her purse for later and she was ready to go. A quick glance in the mirror on her way out of the room and she smiled behind her mask. *Definitely model ready*, she thought. *Time to go to work*.

The elevator door opened. A masked person stood in each corner. She stepped back to wait for the next car. No use getting picked up for violating crowding rules before she left the hotel.

A few minutes later she hit the sidewalk, heels clicking on the concrete. More people hurried along than she expected, many without masks. Darlene shrugged. The latest news reports claimed that masks were pointless since almost everyone had been exposed to the virus already. No one took the news seriously. A cure for the disease? Sure, but it had painful side effects. A vaccine? It took three days of quarantine after the shot for it to be effective. So much damage had been done by the higher ups that you couldn't sort out what to believe anymore. Most people didn't even try. They just accepted that they would eventually fall victim to the virus and die, or if they lived they would catch it again later.

She followed the crowd, turning to follow the younger men as the crowd separated. In a few minutes she found the bar.

She paid her cover after they scanned her forehead for temperature, and stalked her way inside. The neon blue dress she wore stood out among the many red and black dresses on the women within. Individual tables stood the appropriate six feet apart. The few couples dancing were a lot closer than the tables, but everyone had their masks on. A small group of guys eyed her as they sucked their beer from paper cups with paper straws run up under their masks.

One winked at her, pulling his mask up to take a swig direct from his cup. Average looking, but bold.

She winked back and clicked her way over. "Hi, I'm Darlene." She stopped five feet away, then stepped in a little more.

"I'm Bill." He waggled his eyebrows at her. His friends encouraged him with hoots and muffled hisses that might have been a try at whistles.

Yes, she thought. *This was the right group. Bold enough to skirt the law, still trying to wolf whistle. A high chance that they knew where a party could be found.*

She chatted with them a while, then asked Bill to dance. They reached toward each other, never quite touching until they finally bumped elbows.

"Hey, no touching allowed."

Darlene rolled her head dramatically and then looked over her shoulder at the heckler, head tilted slightly down and eyebrows lifted.

"Yeah, you heard me. Don't put the rest of us at risk."

"Like anyone would bother to put *you* at risk." She shook her head and turned back to Bill. "You know a better place to go dancing tonight?"

Bill raised his cheeks and squinted. "Well, we heard about this party…"

"Sounds great. Let's go."

Half an hour later they pulled up in a cul-de-sac filled with cars. Bill maneuvered back to the next street to park. His buddies parked behind them and piled out of their car. They held back a little, allowing Bill and Darlene to precede them.

Another couple approached, maskless. They knocked once and entered, closing the door behind them.

Bill yanked his mask off, stuck it in the pocket of his jeans, and grinned. Darlene stuffed hers in her purse, taking a moment to apply her lipstick. They entered, closely followed by Bill's friends.

Darlene looked around the packed room. Well over the twenty people allowed to gather, not a mask in sight, and music blaring from another room. She peeked inside. Another group, far more than twenty, danced and whirled each other around by the hand, arm, and waist. She drew Bill into the music room, dancing in forbidden close contact for almost twenty minutes before she excused herself for the rest room.

Once inside, she pulled her phone from her purse. "Sheila, I need Trace. I'll leave the line open." She dropped the phone back into her purse, then rejoined Bill on the dance floor.

About fifteen minutes later someone left and then ran back inside. "Drones! The cops are here!"

A few people dashed for the door, only to be tased by the drones waiting outside. One drone buzzed its way through the open door. Its speaker crackled. "You are all under arrest for violating the crowd control act for residential gatherings. Please remain inside until you are directed by officers."

Before long, the police ushered them into three buses with darkened windows.

The Processing Center was located in an old repurposed warehouse. Masked medical workers took their temperatures, drew blood, and separated people into small groups. Darlene removed her clothes when asked and uncovered the tattoo on her right shoulder. A UV scanner found and registered her barcode, hidden inside the bee's stripes, identifying her as a natural immune.

"So what's the count?"

The nurse checked her tablet. "Sixty-three this time. Forty-seven have the virus, but only three have any antibodies. One of the clear ones shows signs of being another immune. They'll hate us all, of course."

"I know. I had enough trouble being stung by a honeybee when I was young. I can't imagine murder hornet venom." Darlene shuddered as she pulled a set of scrubs and matching mask on.

"We'll have them for a week and a half, three days for the venom cure and then a week for the vaccine."

"So Mother Nature's taking care of us? Seems awfully coincidental."

"Well, some of the news reports link the hornets with the same area that first reported the virus. But who believes the news, anyway?" The nurse waved over an orderly. "Walk her over to the cure injection room, wait five minutes, and then walk her down to the dormitories. Make sure she is seen in the hallway."

"Party crasher, huh? Good luck, Miss. One of you saved my younger brother. He had a particularly nasty version of the virus."

Darlene smiled beneath her mask, and made certain to moan and cry after her visit to the injection room. After the police finally released the group, she would break up with Bill over the trauma and move on to her next assignment. *I wonder what state they will send me to this time.*

SILVER SURFER

By Lindsay Lake

What the hell are you doing in my lost
Hobokin town of 7-Eleven? Did you slide from
the slipstream? Did your winged chariot break
down? Did you fall from heavens, shot out by
Venus blast? I've never seen muscles like
yours up close and personal - off the big
screen, that is. Your tan skin and bleached out
hair on your Herculean legs glow silver star
flakes from Atlantis. I swear, I'm taking
surf lessons the rest of my natural born
life – to see you again. Your hair in a man
bun like Sampson; I'd give my young life if
you'd let it down, let it down! Shave, put on
a tux and dance with me till time explodes.

SKIN

By Holly Coop

Race is something we run
Not a description of
Skin

We are all part of a
Human race
We
Are
All
Kin

We were all created
By a power that is pure love
How then can we be against one another?
We are all sisters
We are all brothers
We all have fathers
We all have mothers
We are all children
Created by a power of Love

Until we see ourselves
In our neighbors face
Looking past religion, gender, race
Accept that the same red blood
Runs through veins under every color of
Skin

Each of us is an instrument
A conduit to divine love
We are to treat one another equally
No matter the color of
Skin

We are human beings
Not defined by
Skin

We all run in the same race
We
Are
All
Kin

THE BEST PERSON EVER

By James Pressler

Joey drummed his fingers against the desk, eager to read his report to the class. This assignment had been too much fun, and he was bursting to share his work and make his grandma – Nana – proud. Their teacher, frumpy Ms. Brady, has tasked everyone in the fourth-grade class to write about who they thought was the best person in their life and why, then read it to the class. Joey wanted this moment more than ever, and not just to brag about his grandmother.

He knew people in this little farm town didn't like his grandmother, but he had no idea why. Nana kept to herself just past the tracks, reading and knitting and teaching Joey everything about the world. He loved his Nana dearly but could not figure out why nobody even talked about her, much less referred to her as anyone other than "that Old Lady Garretty." Now, everyone would know just what made Nana the best person ever, starting with his fourth-grade class. Ms. Brady would know why; Principal Booker, leaning next to the chalkboard scratching his dark beard, would know why – everyone would find out just how wonderful Joey's Nana was.

Ms. Brady looked at her class roster. "And the next report is from Joey Garretty."

Joey bounced out of his chair and rushed to the front of the class. Scotty Booker, the class bully and Principal Booker's only child, stuck out a foot and tripped Joey, sending him sprawling across the floor, papers flying through the air. Scotty laughed the loudest out of the entire class while his father looked away, shaking his head in quiet disapproval.

Embarrassment would not stop Joey. He snatched up his papers and went up by Ms. Brady, facing the class with a bright smile and his wonderful revelations written across three sheets of paper. Ms. Brady nodded for him to proceed.

"For my assignment to write about the best person in my life, I wrote about my Nana. Her name is Agnes Garretty, and she was born before this town even had a train stop."

Ms. Brady rested her head in her hands, a sigh filling the air. Principal Booker shook his head. Scotty shouted, "Boo!" from the front row. Joey ignored their bad attitudes. Nothing would stop him from making his Nana proud.

"Nana taught me a lot of important things. She taught me to always be good to people, even if they are bad to you. When she was eighteen years old, the people in this town ex... excomm... excommunicated her from the church. She told me that she never got mad at those people. She knew that if people were really bad, then bad things happened to them. When the people in town forced her to move out, she never complained. She moved to her farmhouse just outside town, and never got upset not once. The next year, when all the grass in the church cemetery died, Nana said this is what happened to bad people. When the church altar burst into flames during Christmas services that year, she reminded me to never be bad, because bad things happen to bad people all the time."

With a quick step, Ms. Brady walked up to Joey. "That's a nice report," she said in clear discomfort. "You can sit..."

"There's more!" Joey flipped to another page. "Nana told me that people who hate me for who I am are bad people, and I should never hate other people if they act differently or do different things. Nana said the farmers around her house never wanted her having her Halloween bonfire parties in the woods with all her friends. She said they were the bad ones, and that bad things would be what they deserved. When Mr. Eggert got killed by his own pigs, it was because he was bad. And when Old Man Coulson got that disease that rotted off his..."

"Joey, that's enough." Ms. Brady brought out both hands to push Joey back toward the class, but he slipped away and continued reading. "My Nana was even nice enough to help me with the report, because she wanted everyone to know what kind of woman she was and the things she could..."

"Now, Joey, you know that's not true," Principal Booker said from his spot leaning against the chalkboard. "Everyone here knows that your... Nana... passed away last year."

"She still helped me!" Joey put down his papers defiantly.

"Before she died, she told me I could talk to her any time. I just needed to hold her special Bible with the black velvet cover, and sit in the moonlight, and we could talk. And we do. And she helped me."

Ms. Brady looked awkwardly at the principal then went toward her rebellious student, hands extended. "Joey, do you know what the punishment is for telling fibs in class?"

"This isn't a fib! She talks to me! She tells me secrets!" Joey scampered back around the desk, staying just out of Ms. Brady's reach. "She's told me secrets about you! She told me that you have a lady friend in the next town and you two have naked sleepovers on the weekends."

Ms. Brady stumbled then caught herself against the edge of her own desk. "What... what do... that's all a misunderstanding. I just... we only... that's a lie!"

The class started laughing as Joey stated his case. "And Nana told me what happens to all the stray cats around Dr. Fletcher's farm and what he does to them."

"You're making this up!" Scotty yelled over the class. "Joey Garretty's a liar. He's a big fat liar! Boo!"

"Yeah?" Joey took a step toward Scotty, past a flabbergasted Ms. Brady. "My Nana told me that Principal Booker isn't really your father, and he knows it and your mom knows it and everyone knows it but you. Your real father is a guy your mom played with behind the church."

Principal Booker braced himself against the chalkboard. "Where did you hear that?"

"Nana said it! And she said you know it's true because you can't have kids and you never wanted them!"

From behind his dark beard, the principal went pale, looking away from the boy and Ms. Brady, who now sat in her chair with trembling hands.

"We're just friends..." she muttered over and over.

Even the students fell quiet, tension whisking them into silence. Scotty Booker ran out of the class in tears, followed by a stunned Principal Booker.

The class now looked at Joey, who returned to his place in front of the teacher's desk and picked up his papers. "So that's why my Nana is the best person ever. She taught me to never be bad because bad things always happen to bad people."

Beaming with pride, Joey returned to his desk. Nobody clapped or laughed. Ms. Brady only wrung her hands. Joey knew everyone in class now saw his Nana a whole new way. Everyone knew the kind of person she really was now, and even though she died last year, Joey felt that Nana just taught everyone a very valuable lesson.

THE CHILD PRODIGY

By Denise M. Baran- Unland

Enjoy an excerpt from the second book in the BryonySeries young adult vampire trilogy "Visage."
For the full book description, visit bryonyseries.com.

Although a month premature, John-Peter passed his first medical exams, and after less than a week in the hospital, Dr. pronounced him healthy enough to go home.

"Keep him away from crowds for the first month," he said, "and bring him to my office in a week for another check-up."

Their first family ride home tinged bittersweet with the unexpected death of Debbie Polis hovering over Melissa's head. Why hadn't John-Peter's mother taken better care of herself? And why had Derek waited until Debbie seized before acting? Her swollen appearance magnified the urgency for medical help.

As if sensing Melissa's thoughts John said, "They're waking Debbie tomorrow night right here in Jenson. I think we should go."

Melissa almost cheered John's proposal. Despite the callous and condescending "holding tank," remarks, John's sense of decency had prevailed. Then Melissa recalled the final instructions.

"Dr. Rothgard told us to keep John-Peter away from crowds. You're not suggesting we leave him with a babysitter."

"Of course not. He can stay in the heated car. We'll enter the funeral home by turns."

John carried the still-sleeping baby up the back steps and into the hushed and still house. With great reverence, John laid the baby in the cradle by his side of the bed. John-Peter grimaced in his sleep, and John steadied him with one hand. John-Peter's breathing faded into the soft sighs of baby sleep. Melissa smiled as she watched him dream. Because of Debbie's tremendous sacrifice, Melissa's most sublime dreams had become euphoric reality.

Leaving the bedroom door ajar, the new parents walked back to the kitchen, where John rummaged in the refrigerator for the ingredients to make a quick meal. Then he faced her with outstretched arms and said, "Come here."

Melissa rushed to meet them and laid her head over John's heart. Its beating never failed to thrill her, a constant reminder that John still lived and shared that life with her. John wrapped one arm around her waist and stroked her hair with his other hand as he rested his chin on her head.

"Well, Melissa, we did it. We're a...."

A piercing cry interrupted John's sentence. John-Peter had awakened and demanded to be fed. Melissa giggled and grabbed a bottle from the electric warmer on the counter.

"While you're making dinner," Melissa said, "I'll tend to our son."

By the time Melissa had reached the bedroom, John-Peter's face was scrunched purple, and he was frantically waving his tiny, clenched fists. She set the bottle on the nightstand and lifted her small squirming son from his bed.

"It's all right, John-Peter," Melissa said in her most soothing tone.

The baby, however, refused her comforting efforts. She tightened her grip on the writhing infant with one hand and reached for the bottle with the other one. John-Peter chomped down on the nipple, drained the milk in seconds, and howled for more. Melissa carried the crying baby into the kitchen.

"John, he still seems hungry."

He lowered the heat and covered the pot with a lid. "Give him another bottle. Dr. Rothgard said to feed him on demand."

"Isn't that too much formula at one time?"

John shrugged. "I don't know. Maybe he didn't receive enough in the hospital."

She had to do something. John-Peter was frantic. Melissa took a second bottle from the warmer and sat at the kitchen table to feed him. The baby accepted this feeding much slower than the last one and soon drifted to sleep. With a napkin, Melissa dabbed the dribbles from the corners of his mouth.

John pulled biscuits from the oven and then tossed the salad. "Dinner's ready. Shall I return him to the cradle?"

"I'll do it."

146

Gingerly, Melissa carried the sleeping baby back to the bedroom. This time, he did not stir when she set him down. She hoped John-Peter would stay asleep, at least until she and John finished dinner.

He lit a candle and opened a bottle of cabernet for the occasion. After Melissa settled in her chair, John raised his glass. "To the Simotes family!"

Melissa clinked hers against his. "Yes, oh, yes!"

They made it only halfway through dinner when John-Peter once again bellowed. Melissa started to rise, but John objected. "My turn. Sit and eat."

"He can't be hungry!"

"I doubt it. Quite possibly, he's lonely."

But the baby continued to wail though the closed bedroom door. Melissa helplessly picked at her creamed chicken.
John returned for another bottle and said, "I'm baffled. It's as if he's starving. Call Dr. Rothgard."

He leaned against the counter and tilted the bottle to the baby's lips. John-Peter slurped its contents and resumed crying before Melissa had finished dialing. John held John- Peter near his shoulder and patted his back.

"Hold on," the receptionist said to Melissa. "He's just walking out the door."

Melissa cupped her hand over the receiver to drown the baby's cries. John gently jiggled the baby. Despite Melissa's frantic recounting, Dr. Rothgard seemed unconcerned with the baby's supposed crisis.

"Have you burped him? Sometimes babies confuse air in their stomachs with hunger."

"John did, but he's still acting hungry."

"For tonight, give him what he wants. Bring him to the office tomorrow. I'm sure there's a simple explanation for it." Melissa hung up the phone and relayed the information to John. He reached for a bottle while Melissa prepared another batch of formula for the warmer.

"Well," she said, "I know parenting's a hard job, but I thought we'd have a day to get used to it."

After consuming his fourth bottle, John-Peter once again fell asleep. Melissa began rinsing the dishes, but John stopped her when he returned from the bedroom.

"I'll clean up," he said. "You take a shower while you have the chance."

John, too, made it to the shower before John-Peter woke again. Remembering Dr. Rothgard's advice, Melissa first burped the baby before giving him yet another bottle. John-Peter sucked it dry by the time an incredulous John had emerged from the bathroom.

"He can't be hungry!"

Melissa grinned. "I'm so glad you're taking the middle of the night feeding."

John frowned. "If this continues, neither of us will sleep."

Once Melissa settled John-Peter in his cradle, he showed no signs of disturbing his parents. Melissa gazed at her sleeping son as John turned back the bedcovers.

"John, he's so sweet. He looks like an angel."

He climbed into bed and patted the empty place beside him. Only with difficulty did Melissa resist the urge to continue gazing at the little, cherubic face. Nevertheless, John had one or two urges of his own, and he exploded when John-Peter interrupted with a shriek, and Melissa broke away to fetch him.

"Melissa, he's fine!"

"He's a new baby!"

Melissa flew out of bed and paced the floor with the still-screaming infant as John glared at her. "Maybe, he should just cry for a while."

"I didn't know you believed in letting babies cry!" Melissa shouted over the din.

"I don't."

John-Peter chewed on his fists. Blinking back tears, Melissa left the room for a bottle. Why couldn't John understand she felt disappointed, too? She switched on the kitchen light, opened the warmer, and grabbed yet another bottle while John-Peter bawled in her ear. Melissa started crying, too. As she sat on the chair to feed the baby, she felt John's hand lightly touch her shoulder.

"I'll take him," John said. "Go rest."

The bed's emptiness reminded her of last summer, when John, in his misery over his infertility, had forsaken it. She crawled under the rumpled sheets, jammed her pillow overhead, and cried until she drifted to sleep. When she awakened, the luminous numbers in the lightening room read six o'clock. Melissa felt John's side of the bed. It was still empty. Deafening silence engulfed the house. Holding her breath, Melissa turned the doorknob and eased open the door. She tiptoed into the living room, pausing at each creak of the floor. John, feet propped on the coffee table, head back, and baby on his chest, was lightly snoring. A pile of empty bottles lay on the floor next to the chair.

Melissa had no experience with newborns, but one thing she certainly knew. No baby should go through that much food. She couldn't wait for Dr. Rothgard to fix the problem.

But Dr. Rothgard gave them startling news. "John-Peter's lost weight."

"What!" John said. "That's impossible!" "How much did you say he ate yesterday?"

"Over a hundred ounces, at least," Melissa said.

Dr. Rothgard scrawled something Melissa could not read, tore it from the pad, and gave it to Melissa. John, hands slightly shaking, began diapering the baby.

"Don't give him anymore formula than this...." Dr. Rothgard began.

"He'll just cry for more," Melissa said.

As if on cue, John-Peter screamed. John rummaged in the diaper bag for a bottle.

"Let me finish. In between feedings, feed him some rice cereal if he seems hungry. Give him all the water he'll accept. Bring him back next week to check his weight, sooner if you're concerned."

New Year's Eve traffic jammed the roads; John-Peter's inconsolable crying jarred her nerves. Twice, John's eyes closed during the short trip home, and twice Melissa offered to take the wheel. John-Peter finally fell asleep when John turned onto their street. The baby did not wake up when John slid him out of the car seat nor after John lay him down in the cradle. John sat on the bed to remove his shoes and fell asleep, sitting straight up.

Melissa returned to the kitchen, reading the directions for the rice cereal. She wanted to be ready when John-Peter awakened. When she returned to the bedroom to ready for bed, John had passed out.

Because Melissa did not wish to disturb him, she snuggled into her chair with a novel. Soon, John-Peter's crying woke her. As Melissa rubbed her eyes, she saw John stumble from the bedroom carrying their wailing son. By the time Melissa reached the kitchen, John was sitting on a chair feeding John-Peter a bottle. Yawning, Melissa opened the box of rice cereal. After the baby ate half its contents, he finally dropped off to sleep.

Exhausted, Melissa's eyes fell on the stove clock. Midnight. John rose from the table with the baby, smiled, and kissed Melissa's forehead.

"Happy first anniversary, Melissa," he said.

At dawn, John-Peter drank three bottles of formula and polished off the rest of the cereal. John left the house to search for a store still open on a holiday. Two hours later, he returned with a case of formula and three more boxes of rice cereal. The cereal slowed John-Peter's appetite, as Dr. Rothgard promised it would, and improved his sleep and his disposition, but the baby did eat two boxes of it, as well as half the formula.

"We go back to Shelby in the morning," John said.

The next day, when Dottie Sherman laid John-Peter on the scale, she said, "He's lost another ounce."

Stunned, Melissa looked up at John and then back at Nurse Sherman. *"How?"*

"Aren't you feeding him?"

"Enough for ten babies," John retorted.

"Well, you can discuss that with the doctor."

THE GARBAGE MAN

By Tom Hernandez

"So, you admit you're guilty?"

Officer Paul George had only started his interview, yet his scowl made it clear his patience was already paper-thin. But Nelson Edwards had never been in a police department before. He took a minute to look around. Six officers, both uniformed and in plain clothes, sat at or stood over desks, chatting about new and old arrests and active cases. Computer keyboards softly transferred information to the glowing desktop screens. One antique Selectric typewriter clacked away in a far corner of the room, operated by a cop who appeared to be as much an antique as the device. Radios blurted static-laced cop lingo. A wall clock reading 9 o-clock hung on a wall painted a flat, dull, bureaucratic gray green.

Finally, the officer broke the silence. "Well?"

He stared at George for a second. "This is different than what I expected."

"What?"

"The station," Nelson said. "I mean, I've never seen the inside of a police station. Ever. For anything. Heck, I've never even really talked to a cop until I met you tonight. No speeding tickets, no insurance reports. Nothing."

"I'm glad to hear you've been such an upstanding citizen up 'til now," George said. The corners of his tired eyes crinkled with not-so-subtle sarcasm.

"It's not that, it's just that my only image of the police has come from television – you know, blaring sirens, hookers lined up on a bench, drunks throwing up in a cell."

"Well this may come as a surprise to you, Mr. Edwards, but television isn't always accurate. Not even those so-called reality shows."

"Oh, I know that." Nelson laughed at what he took to be the cop's attempt at humor.

George's sharp stare and what sounded like a growl confirmed in no uncertain terms Nelson had misunderstood.

"Alright now Johnny Clean Cut, knock off the BS and answer my question," George demanded. "Do you admit you're guilty of shooting the victim?"

Nelson took a deep breath and considered his options. "Look, I am many things, but I am not one to lie. I believe the truth is always the best route…"

"Well I am so glad to hear that…"

"…and the truth is, I shot the guy…"

"Ok, now we're getting somewhere…"

"…but that doesn't mean I'm guilty."

George looked at Nelson again like he'd just flicked him in the ear.

"What *does* that mean, exactly?"

Nelson paused a split second, trying to put his thoughts in an order that would hopefully make as much sense to the cop as to himself. "It means that I shot him. But 'guilt' is a philosophical expression of regret for one's actions. And I don't regret shooting him at all. Not one bit."

George guffawed. "Wow! I haven't heard that much semantic mumbo-jumbo since my Ethics 101 class in college!"

"Forgive me, but you're wrong," Nelson said, modulating his tone of voice, not wanting to throw more gas on a potential fire. "This isn't just semantics," he continued. "I am very deliberate with my words. I work hard to say exactly what I mean, and to mean exactly what I say. And what I mean is, I shot him, but I felt – feel – entirely justified."

"Justified or not, it's still illegal. You can't just go around shooting people just because they do something you don't like. We don't want or need any of that movie vigilante nonsense."

"Now wait just a minute!" Nelson rose quickly, forgetting his right hand was cuffed to the chair back. The chair tipped forward, banging against the desk. Every officer in the room instinctively spun toward the metallic clang. Several dropped to their knees and simultaneously drew their guns.

George quickly waved his hands toward the wall of blue that had formed. "Stand down, everyone, stand down," he said. "It's alright," he reassured, order now restored. "Just a moment of insanity on Mr. Edwards' part. It's passed. We're all good."

152

Nelson stood still as a statue, not daring to breath or even blink until all the officers re-holstered their firearms. He trusted the police, generally speaking. As much as anyone else who never encountered them. Still, he'd seen all the news stories about rogue cops shooting young black men to maintain a healthy dose of life-preserving doubt. Not that he was young or black, but it never hurts to be careful, he reminded himself. They slowly turned back to their paperwork. One or two focused a cautious eye in his direction for several minutes.

"Well, I have to say, *that* looked a lot more like television." Nelson smiled involuntarily, exhaled and sat down gingerly. "I'm sorry. I didn't mean to cause a fuss. I just want it clear that I had a very good reason for doing what I did."

"Fine." George took his pen back into his left hand and hovered it over the yellow legal pad slanted across his desk. "Understand I'm not making any legal judgments, but for the sake of moving this along, I'll take you at your word. Now tell me exactly what happened."

"Mom, where are you?"

"I'm up here, honey. Hold on, I'll be right down." Helen quickly folded the last few items in the laundry basket, laid them on the appropriate dressers for herself and Nelson and bounded down the stairs.

Melissa scolded her mother. "Hey, be careful! You're not a spring chicken anymore."

"Ha, ha, very funny," Helen said. She wrapped her arms around her oldest daughter and held her tightly, her chin resting easily on the younger woman's shoulder. "It's amazing, but you still smell the same now at twenty-three as you did when you were a baby."

Melissa gently broke the hug and laughed. "I certainly hope not, considering what I spent on this perfume, and knowing how bad babies can smell sometimes."

"You know what I mean," Helen said. She smiled gently at her daughter, now a grown woman. "You'll understand someday when you're a mother."

"Well, I am not interested in having a baby any time soon so it may be a while." Melissa returned her mother's smile, love lighting her eyes. "Where's Dad?"

"Your father? I don't know."

"You don't know? You guys didn't have a fight, did you?"

"No! Not at all." Helen sat on the couch and patted the spot next to her. Melissa wedged herself into the corner of the couch and turned to face her mom. "I mean, he went for a walk about an hour ago and I haven't heard from him."

Melissa's eyes crossed the living room to the family dog who lay snoring on his oversize pillow bed near the television. "Doesn't he usually take Duncan with him?"

"Usually," Helen said, "but not always. Sometimes he just goes off by himself."

Melissa looked over her mother's shoulder at the graying sky in the picture window. "This late? It's getting dark out there."

"Sweetie, I understand, but after nearly forty years, I don't ask anymore." Helen chuckled. "That's something else you'll learn if you're very, very lucky." She rolled her eyes. Melissa laughed sympathetically. She understood her father's idiosyncrasies well enough to know why her mother sometimes opted for blissful ignorance.

"Seriously, I'm not concerned. Your dad just needs some time and room to burn off whatever fog is in his head," Helen said. "He's a good man and he's earned that much. The only thing that bothers me is, sometimes he seems more upset when he comes back. Well, that and his outfit."

"His outfit?"

"Yes. Once in a while, especially when he goes out later in the day like this, he wears his black sweatshirt and sweatpants. I'm always worried that he's going to get hit by a car crossing the street or walking down that path through the park. You know how dark it gets in there under those trees. I've told him and told him to wear something easier for people to see, but you know your father. You can't tell him anything."

Officer George raised his pen above his yellow legal pad, already graffiti-ed with indecipherable notes. "OK, start from the beginning."

"Um…" Nelson's eyes fell to the pad and rose again to George's face.

"What is it, Mr. Edwards?"

"Well, are you going to *write* down my statement? As opposed to *typing* it, I mean?"

George's forehead wrinkled with confusion. "What?"

"Not to cast aspersions," Nelson said. "I mean, my handwriting is atrocious too. It's so bad that sometimes I can't read what I wrote later, and I just want to make sure you get this right."

"Listen, Mr. Edwards," George said, not a sliver of patience offered or even hinted. "Not that it makes any difference to you, but I am not a great typist. I write now, type later. I'm kind of 'old school' that way. Plus, you will get a chance to review everything before I ever put fingers on the keyboard. I have been a police officer for twenty-four years now, and every single second of my twenty-four years of experience is strongly suggesting you focus a little more on what you're going to say and a little less on how I am going to write it down."

The cop made a show of gently laying the offending pen on the notepad. Then he turned slightly from Nelson, took a handkerchief from his back pocket and wiped a speck of spittle from the corner of his lips. He turned back and raised the pen again, his now-clean lips smiling. "Can we do this now?"

Nelson lowered his head and laughed a little to himself. "Yes, sir. Really, there's not much to tell. A couple nights ago, I went to the park near my house to take a walk as I do every night. And there was garbage all over the path, in the bushes and flower beds, everywhere. Just like every night. Dirty paper plates. Styrofoam takeout boxes. Fast food bags and cups – and not always empty, either. Plastic water bottles. Beer cans and booze bottles in the grass. Broken glass on the sidewalks where kids walk to the elementary school – the elementary school, for goodness sakes!" Nelson shook his head.

George cut him off. "And what? This made you mad enough to go back tonight and shoot someone?"

"Well, not exactly."

"Well, what, *exactly*?" George pressed.

"The garbage made me mad, sure. So did the fact that I called the city seven times and asked them to either come clean it up or have the police do a better job patrolling the park" – Nelson quickly caught himself – "present company excluded of course..."

"Of course."

"No, what really made me mad, and not just this time, but every night for weeks, months, heck the last couple of years since I've started walking each night, is that there are garbage cans every two or three hundred yards along the path." Nelson started to rise again but he quickly checked the impulse as the other officers pivoted toward his voice.

George took up Nelson's story. "So, you put on dark clothes, hid in the underbrush along the path, waited there until someone came along and littered, and you shot him. Is that it?"

Nelson paused. The words sounded silly coming out of the cop's mouth. Frivolous. But Nelson knew to the core of his being, that he was right, no matter how ridiculous things appeared. "Right," he said simply.

"Fine," George exhaled as if he'd won a battle.

Nelson looked back at the clock on the wall. He couldn't believe he'd been there an hour already. "No!" Nelson said, not even bothering to try to contain his contempt now. "I shot him because he has no respect. Not for the law, or the environment or for society. Not for our community and the neighborhood we all share. Most of all, for anyone else. They're selfish and lazy. Pigs, every one of them. They think the world is theirs and they're the only ones in it."

George stared at Edwards, waiting for him to say something he could legally explain, if not outright defend.

"I mean, there is so much ugliness in this world. People hurting their kids and their spouses. Bullying everywhere. Politicians dividing us so they can conquer each other. Religious hypocrites hating and rejecting anyone who dares to believe something different from them," Nelson explained.

"I get all that, but..."

156

"No buts! No more buts!" Nelson slammed his free hand on George's desk. He took a breath, struggling again to contain his temper, handcuffs and police officers and guns and jail cells be damned. "I mean, it's not that hard! Put your goddamn trash in the cans! Is that so much to ask?"

"Look, most of the time I simply pick up what I can and throw it away," Nelson said, somewhat sheepishly. "I tell myself that bending over fifty times a mile is good cardio. But I decided a couple days ago that I've had enough. Just like in the movie: 'I am mad as hell, and I am not going to take it anymore!'"

George stared at Nelson. "What are you talking about?"

"*Network,*" Nelson said. "The classic film? You've never seen it?"

"Sorry," George said. "No."

Nelson shook his head and continued. "Look, I'm a simple guy. I don't ask for much. I try to be a good neighbor. I help at church. I don't live high off the hog. My wife and I, we're not flashy. We have a nice, little house that we built into a home first for us, then for our kids, now for our grand kids."

"Oh, you have grandchildren?"

"Not yet, but maybe someday. And when we do, guys like me, we just want to be able to enjoy whatever time we have left in a world that doesn't laugh at us or spit in our faces."

Officer George reflexively reached for his handkerchief again, but Nelson waved him off. "No, you're fine. I wasn't talking about you. I'm talking about the guy I shot, and everyone like him."

"So, did you know this person?"

"No. But why does that even matter? He's the same as all the rest of these jerks who can't even take the time to give two craps about anyone else. I don't know him, same as he doesn't know me. But we shouldn't have to *know* someone to care for them, to respect their place in the world. We all share a little bit of space in this world. Yet he has no problem violating that space which, for a guy like me, is sacred. I just want a place in my tiny little corner that's safe and clean and quiet. Someplace I can go to get away from all the other crap in the world today without having to step over piles of garbage."

Nelson slumped back into the chair. As usual, the relief of honesty made him feel palpably lighter. Officer George scribbled furiously, fighting to capture every word of Nelson's statement. Finally, he stopped writing and stared at the page. After what seemed like minutes of silence, he looked up at the captive culprit.

"Mr. Edwards, no one will ever mistake me for one of those left-wing tree hugger types, but I do enjoy the outdoors every now and again, so I understand your frustration with litter -- "

"No sir, not with litter. With the litter *bugs*." Nelson purposely lowered his voice.

"Right." The cop dutifully wrote 'B-U-G-S' in the margin of his notepad, then pointed at the page. "Got it. Litter bugs. Either way, like I said before, you can't just go around shooting people who do things you don't like."

Nelson sensed the hammer was about to fall. He stared into his lap.

"I get where you're coming from," George continued, "but I have to charge you with something."

"Like what?" Nelson asked, hoping he wouldn't spend too much time behind bars.

"All things considered, and especially since the guy wasn't really hurt, we're probably looking at a misdemeanor of some kind."

Nelson took a breath, one-part relief, one-part confusion, one-part suspicion. "Just a misdemeanor? What's the penalty?"

"Depends. Judge's discretion. Could be a $500 fine, could be community service."

"Community service? Like what?"

"Usually, picking up trash," George said. It was his turn to try to stifle a laugh. "You're just lucky it was only a paintball gun."

"No, *he's* lucky it was just a paintball gun!" Nelson snapped, then quickly caught himself. "Well of course it was just a paintball gun. I may be mad, but I'm not crazy. I didn't want to hurt anyone, I just wanted to teach someone a lesson. He's lucky I didn't paint a big 'LB' on his chest."

Once again, George offered only a blank stare.

"Like in *The Scarlet Letter*?" Nelson prodded. "Hester Prynne? Reverend Arthur Dimmesdale? C'mon, really? You *must* know the *Scarlet Letter*. Where did you go to school anyway?"

George cocked his right eyebrow. "Mr. Edwards, please don't push your luck."

"No sir. I mean, yes sir."

Nelson looked back at the wall clock. Another thirty minutes had evaporated. He realized he hadn't called his wife. Officer George had started filling a form on his computer. "Sir, I never did get my one phone call."

Officer George nodded toward his desk phone, his eyes locked on the screen as two fingers hunted and pecked on the keyboard. "Feel free," he said.

"Um, sir, I can't reach..." Nelson rattled his cuffed right hand.

"You're pushing again, Mr. Edwards."

Helen answered the chiming phone.

"Nelson? Honey, where are you? Melissa is here. She's been waiting for you since just after you left. We thought maybe you got lost. You *are* getting older, you know." She looked at her daughter and smiled at her gibe and started to roll her eyes again.

Her eyes suddenly stopped, mid-roll. "What? Where? The *police* station*?"* Helen said.

"What's wrong Mom? Is Dad OK?"

Helen shook her head and held up a finger to Melissa. "What in the world...What did you do?"

Nelson gripped the receiver with his free left hand. He looked at Officer George still slowly completing on his report. He debated for a second how to answer. He wanted to be honest but not alarm her.

Just then, another officer escorted a tall, twenty-something man across the other end of the office toward the holding pen. The young man was a rainbow of blue and green and pink and red and orange and yellow quarter and half-dollar sized splotches, some still dripping down his grimy shirt and torn jeans. Nelson caught the man's eye and glowered at him until the cell door clicked shut.

"Let's just say I was taking out the trash."

THE VOICES

By Holly Coop

TINY LITTLE VOICES
CRYING OUT IN TUNE
WAITING TO BE HEARD
BY A NATION GONE ASKEW

THE WORDS THEY SHOUT IN THEIR SILENCE
HEARD ONLY BY THE HEARTS OF SOME
ARE REAL DESPITE THE MANY
WHO *CHOOSE* TO PLAY DEAF AND DUMB

i may not be born
but my heart does still beat
in this hidden place within my mother's womb
my lungs work
i can suck my thumb
and wiggle the toes on my feet

though i have yet to take my first breath
i am your bone
i am your flesh
i can hear
and i feel

when will this nation treat me,
and the millions of others too
with dignity
we have the same God given rights
as grownups do
ADMIT THE TRUTH
*we **are** human beings*
just like you

the only difference is a mother

who chooses for her child
life
but many choose
death
for the child they carry inside

they think it is all right
*they have **all** been fed a lie*
oh if they only knew
they are victims too

killing is still killing
no matter the victim's age
why is it so much easier
when you can't see the person's face

TINY LITTLE VOICES
CRYING OUT IN TUNE
WAITING TO BE HEARD
BY A NATION GONE ASKEW

please go make a difference
the real choice lies with you
give the unborn life
they have a VOICE too

THERE'S NO SUCH THING AS A GHOST

By Denise M. Baran-Unland

Enjoy an excerpt from the first book in the BryonySeries young adult vampire trilogy "Bryony."
For the full book description, visit bryonyseries.com.

A lanky man, about forty, in a green, pocket T-shirt, faded blue jeans, and threadbare gym shoes, was holding a tape measure against her bedroom wall. He reached behind his ear for his pencil, pulled a wrinkled paper from his pocket, and jotted some figures. Glancing up, he noticed Melissa, and his face broke into a wide grin.

"Howdy!" The man shook Melissa's hand. He had an open, friendly face and a shock of blond hair over his forehead. "I'm Steve. Melissa, right?"

She nodded and limply returned the handshake, feeling a little surprised her mother had become sociable with him. Steve was so different from her father, always sophisticated in pressed pants and collared shirt, even at his sickest.

"Your ma tells me you like to read. Soon, you'll have plenty of bookshelves."

Her mother stuck her head around the door. "Steve, I've got hamburgers and hot dogs. Will you stay for dinner?"

"On one condition," Steve said. "I man the grill."

Brian poked his head past, looking hopeful. Steve grinned. "With Brian's help."

His face lit up as he slipped away. Back home, their mother did the cooking and never allowed Brian near an open flame, despite his loud protests, but Steve seemed relaxed around both Brian and fire. He asked Brian's opinion about the amount of charcoal briquettes and trusted Brian's judgment for when the fire was sufficiently hot. Darlene brought out the meat and a foil pan of frozen French fries.

"Now there's a meal fit for a king," Steve said.

He rumpled Brian's hair. Brian glowed, and Melissa relaxed, a little. Maybe, she could unpack a few boxes. She slipped back inside and surveyed the stacks with despair. Where would she put it

162

all? She slowly peeled tape off the first box. It seemed so final, unpacking her things into a new room in a strange house. So, Melissa set her stereo on top of her dresser, just like in her Grover's Park bedroom, added a stack of 45's, and sang with the music, while she stacked stuffed animals in a corner; hung sweaters; and filled dresser drawers with jeans, T-shirts, and socks. She had just made her bed when her mother's voice startled her.

"Melissa." Darlene opened the door a crack. "Dinner time."

"Already?" Melissa scrambled to her feet. How could two hours have passed?

The makeshift dining room was part of the living room. Brian was actually setting the table, a chore he dodged back home.

"It sure looks good," Melissa said. "The food smells good, too."

"Brian did most of the work." Steve set down a platter of hamburgers.

"I'll take another cook," Darlene said, "especially one that washes dishes."

"Whatever!" Brian twisted his face in disgust.

As they ate, Steve asked Melissa if she had seen the property. Memories of the mist rose in her mind, so she hesitated before answering. It figured Brian would blab.

"Liss saw a ghost." Brian tore apart a French fry. "It chased her down the path."

Melissa glared at Brian, but only because he was too far away for her to stomp on his foot.

"Go on, Liss," Brian said, oblivious to her reaction. "Tell him!"

Steve looked skeptically at Melissa. "A ghost?"

Melissa's face grew hot. "I...I don't know what I saw," she stammered. "I was walking by the lake, and suddenly I was covered with this mist."

"The waitress at Sue's Diner said the mansion was haunted," Darlene said, with a dubious look at Melissa. "My kids have overactive imaginations."

"I'm sure Melissa did see something," Steve said, "but that mist was simply cold and warm air mixing, like how clouds are formed. It's common around here."

"I didn't see it," Brian insisted.

"Were you looking for it?"

Brian shook his head, his eyes on Steve.

"Then it was gone by the time Melissa mentioned it. Now, if you had seen the mist in the mansion...." Steve winked at their mother.

Brian smirked at Melissa, and their mother noticed. "There's no mist inside the mansion, Brian," Darlene said.

Steve's tone grew serious. "Folks here might disagree with you. They tell stories of shadows moving in the house and beautiful piano music at night, but that's all they are, bonfire stories. Naturally, there's no such thing as a ghost." Steve poured another glass of iced tea. "So, don't get ideas about ghost chasing. You could get hurt."

Brian stuck his tongue at Melissa, but she was remembering the shadow in the gazebo.

"Not from a ghost," Steve gave Brian a warning look, "but from playing inside an old, dilapidated house. During some preliminary inspections, a workman was injured. Tell your friends, too. Some kids tried biking up there a few weeks ago, and the project manager had to shoo them away."

Friends, Melissa thought bitterly. My friends are back in Grover's Park. I'll probably never have friends again.

Steve noticed Brian's disappointed look. "Now, now. They're starting work this spring. Maybe, then, we can get you a look around the place."

"Okay," Brian agreed.

He nudged Melissa's foot. She peeked underneath. Brian crossed his fingers. How long before Brian stopped thinking about ghosts?

"I know something scarier than ghosts," Darlene said. "School starts next week. We need to go shopping, especially for you Brian. You've outgrown everything."

Brian made a face and groaned. Melissa said nothing, but she detested shopping more than Brian did. She preferred jeans and only wore dresses when necessary.

Steve asked about her mother's writing, so Brian, restless, walked Scooter behind the cottage. Melissa stretched and followed. Scooter sniffed every blade of grass.

"Maybe the mist was John Simons," Brian said, "pining away for his lost love." He fell to his knees, clasped his hands, and fluttered his lashes, just as Laura did when flirting. Scooter licked his face so hard Brian fell backward, and Melissa laughed. She decided against telling Brian about the shadow in the gazebo. It was probably a raccoon. Why fuel the fire?

"Don't be ridiculous. Look at this place. John Simons got bored, went to Europe, and died there. I'm going back inside. It's too dark to see anymore."

The adults were talking about the village's plans for the Simons estate. The renovation of Simons Mansion might bring significant changes to the village, and that excited Steve.

"People do come here to fish, but that's our only real industry," Steve said. "Opening Simons Mansion to the public would give more people reasons to visit us."

"Classical piano fans are a minority," Darlene said. "That won't bring people in."

"Sure it will, if the village plays up the ghost story," Steve said.

Brian sat up straighter.

"People won't fall for it," Darlene insisted.

"They will, and the village board intends to capitalize on it," Steve said. "Munsonville hasn't progressed much in a century, so you almost can't blame them.

"Why don't you believe the stories?" Brian asked.

"I've worked all over the grounds and have never seen or heard anything."

Brian persisted. "Then why do people say there's a ghost?"

"People invent stories when circumstances are unclear. John Simons abruptly left town, leaving behind a huge estate and no heir, so people speculate. Ghost stories are more fascinating than truth, which, sad to say, can be boring. Of course," Steve winked again at their mother, "the kids can make it exciting for the centennial."

"A ghost is exciting." Brian would not give up.

"The ghost is legendary, not historical. Melissa, maybe you'd like to write about John Simons. He's a significant part of Munsonville's history."

Melissa politely nodded her head. She had no interest in Munsonville history, its dead musician, or the mansion, only her father's connection to them.

"If John Simons didn't leave his estate to anyone," Melissa said, "how did my dad get it?"

Steve corrected her. "Your father had only the mansion and part of the grounds. The village owned the rest. Because of private interest, it was impossible to develop a full-scale tourist plan. It's only recently we discovered the owner." He smiled at her mother. "I'm sure glad we did."

Brian wrinkled his nose and gagged. Melissa nudged him with her elbow, but she glanced at her mother and Steve. That's how her father smiled, and she didn't appreciate it on this man's face. To Melissa's annoyance, her mother smiled back. Melissa shifted uncomfortably. Steve noticed, and his smile faded.

"One last thing," Steve said. "The place is full of bryony. John Simons was a fool to plant that weed all over his house and estate. It's a nuisance for me, but that's an artist for you. In the meantime, stay away from any plant you can't identify."

"Is bryony valuable?" Melissa asked. So, bryony was the vines she had noticed.

"No, it's poisonous." Steve tipped his glass to finish the iced tea, and his eyes fell on his watch. "Gosh, I'm sorry! I didn't realize it was late."

"That's quite all right," Darlene said. "We've enjoyed the company. I'll walk you to your truck. Kids, please clear off the table."

As her mother and Steve moved away, Melissa heard Steve say, "It's not right, you and the kids staying in the woods alone...."

Melissa collected the glasses. Brian stood with his hands in his pockets.

"You could help," Melissa said irritably. "Mom wasn't just talking to me, you know."

"Why not write about the ghost? It's still part of the mansion's history."

166

"Steve said a ghost is not history. It's legend." Melissa headed for the kitchen. "Can you, at least, open the door?"

Brian absently turned the knob. "It might become history. Look at what you saw."

"Steve told you what I saw: cold and warm air mixing."

"And you believe him?"

"Steve lives here. I guess he knows what's by the lake. Be quiet. Mom's coming."

Her mother moved slowly. Her face looked wan. She had an early morning meeting at Village Hall, too. Melissa hated housework, but she knew what her father would say, so she hugged her mother, forced a smile, and said, "Get some sleep, Mom. I'll clean up."

Her mother, face softening with relief, kissed Melissa on the forehead and headed to her room. Brian darted off before Melissa could order him into duty. Brothers!

Melissa scraped leftover food into the tiny garbage can under the sink. It would need emptying twice a day, but so what? That was Brian's job. She peered through the window, but night shrouded her view. She only saw her mother's wedding ring on the sill. Detergent residue irritated her skin, so her mother always removed her ring before washing dishes. Once, her mother had knocked the ring down the drain, and Laura's dad had spent an entire afternoon fishing it out.

The soap's foam reminded Melissa of mist, and she shook her head to clear the unpleasant memory. As she soaked the silverware and washed the plastic plates, her mind roamed back to the last night at Pizza Express.

"Tell us about your famous musician," Kimberly Whitney had said, her blue eyes gleaming with uncharacteristic interest. She had always claimed not to wear contacts, but Melissa knew she was lying. Nobody's eyes had color that clear.

In hushed, dramatic tones, Shelly Gallagher told how John Simons had fallen in love with seventeen-year-old Bryony Marseilles, daughter of Munsonville's minister, and had built the mansion in the woods as his wedding present to her. John had also covered the house and filled the grounds with pink-flowered bryony, specially bred for his wife.

167

"Isn't that so romantic?" Shelly had sighed. "She was the same age as us."

Laura Jones had been gawking at Jason, and she blushed and giggled into her pop when he noticed. "Melissa's lucky!" Then she stole another peek at Jason.

Melissa dug through boxes for a towel, still not feeling lucky. She had just dried the last cup when Scooter barked, and she shushed him, wondering what he wanted.

Scooter ran to the living room, so Melissa hung up the towel and followed him to the screen door, where he stood whining. She peered into Brian's room, but her brother was sleeping. Melissa didn't see the leash. Scooter had better not run off.

Melissa opened the patio doors. The overwhelming silence struck her, so different from Grover's Park. There, Melissa often heard cars driving past her house or neighbors talking in their back yards. Here, millions of stars filled the sky, and the moon glowed with golden brilliancy. Her heartbeat fast with indescribable yearning.

Scooter was almost back to the screen door when he stopped, turned around, and froze. His eyes locked onto the woods beyond him. He growled a low, menacing growl. Melissa strained her eyes but saw nothing.

"Silly dog," she scolded him. "It's probably just a rabbit."

Once inside, Melissa refilled Scooter's water and food bowl, then readied for bed, deliberately ignoring the blank walls of her new room. Tomorrow, they would have brand-new shelves, and she would stack all her books. Then would it feel like home?

Melissa switched off the overhead light, felt her way to the nightstand, and groped for her little purple reading light. Propped on her pillow was a ragged, hardbound book, *Nocturnal Lore: The Collected Tales of Henry Matthews*. Obviously, her mother had found it in the cottage and left it for Melissa.

Burrowing under the covers, Melissa opened the book, wrinkling her nose at its moldy smell. She quickly became engrossed in *Flee Unto Dawn*, a story about a young widow who slept each night on her husband's grave, despite the sexton's persistent warning: *Don't squander it on the dead!*

She blinked several times, but her eyelids grew heavy. She yawned, determined to find out what happened to the woman, and carefully turned a crumbling page. She awoke with her head on the book. In the distance was the faint tinkling of piano music. Melissa slid the book under her pillow and turned off the light. Probably someone's car radio, she thought, as she drifted away to sleep.

THIS NATION IS

By Holly Coop

A nation that has lost its good taste

A nation that has lost sight

A nation in desperate need of an end to its many a plight

A nation craving *salt*

A nation deprived of *light*

This nation that has plenty, many fields filled with seed

Wastes the wants of starving children, we fail to feed

Cities filled with skyscrapers stretching from sea to shining sea

Makes no room at the inn for families cast out onto streets

This nation with a God who is the Great Healer

Leave their solders with wounds to bleed

Adding to their suffering-after-suffering, so others could be free

This nation where flags wave for freedom

Many remain un-free

Keeping citizens shackled in a lifetime of poverty

Under the name of aid

Adding linkage to their chains

This nation has lost its sight

This nation has lost good taste

This nation in desperate need of change

TODAY IS NOT A RED BANNER DAY

By S. Houk

Today is not the red banner day.
The shock and awe
Of another you-have-to-shake-and-worry
Newsflash blood pressure bash
Through the color of blood
Across the screen
Top and bottom both
For good measure
Enough blood to go around.
No.
Today is not a red banner day.
Today is a rainy day.
A tree day.
Your problems
And the world's problems
Are my problems
But they occupy
A place.
A blue place
In a green box
On a pink shelf
And I'll open it when I have energy
To contribute to the solution
Never forgetting
The earth is a door
To the outside universe
Where banners of lights
Wave.

WHISPER

By Steven James Cordin

"What did you say to him?" Candles asked as Stilts whispered into the dying man's ear.

Stilts stood and wiped the blood off his switch blade on a rag he pulled from his pocket.

"I told him my real name. I always tell people my name when I kill them. I believe if I take someone's life, they should at least know who is doing it."

Without another word, Stilts bent over and reached under the dead man's arms. Candles studied him for a moment. Weird dude, he thought, if I didn't need the money….

"Quit gawking and get the gate, Candles."

Candles nodded and tried the gate to the auto yard. It was unlocked. He slid it open wide enough for him to walk through and Stilts to drag the body inside.

"Do you think anyone inside the garage saw us?" Stilts pulled the body behind an old Ford.

Candles peered across the yard. It was full of old cars and other junk. The only building, a large old mechanic's garage, was at the other end of the yard.

"No, there is no clear line of sight from the garage and it doesn't look like they had surveillance cameras, which is why that guy was at the gate." Candles knelt behind the Ford and checked his cell phone. "Let's wait here a sec, 'til Rose texts me everything in the back is clear."

Stilts nodded and crouched down next to Candles. He reached into his wind breaker and pulled out a nine-millimeter Beretta.

"Say, why does the boss call you guys Candles and Rose?"

"I dunno. Just names that stuck." He did not bother asking where Stilts got his nickname. The man was well over six feet tall and towered over most people.

The two remained silent for a few moments. Then Candles' phone vibrated.

"Rose got over the fence with no problems," Candles said as he read the display. "There isn't anyone in the yard, must be in the garage. He is waiting for us on the west side."

"Cool."

The two of them skulked across the yard towards the garage, keeping close to the junked cars for cover. As they neared, they saw Rose crouched against the side of the garage.

"Hey guys. I peeked in the back door. The three of them are too busy working on an engine to notice anything out here."

"Sweet." Stilts studied them for a moment. "Okay, here is the plan. Rose will go in through the back door. Wait till Candles pings you on the cell and head in. Candles and I will go in through the main door. We take them out, grab the money and the drugs and go."

"What's our cut?" Rose asked.

"The boss only wants the drugs. We will split the cash between us." Stilts was silent a second and then said. "I figure thirty grand each."

Candles grinned. Thirty thousand would take care of a lot of problems. He would be set for a good long while.

"One more thing." Stilts continued. "Boss wants these bastards dead. Any problems with that?'

174

"Hell, for thirty I'd cap Rose."

"Only if I don't shoot you first." Rose replied and grinned. He stood and said to Candles, "You be careful bro."

"You too, man."

Stilts watched Rose until he disappeared behind the building. "You two have known each other for a while."

"Since high school." Candles replied as he checked his gun. "We been partners for years."

"You are up for this?"

"I need the money. I don't care who we have to kill."

Stilts nodded and started forward. Candles followed him along the side of the building to the main door. It was unlocked. Candles looked through the glass. The lights were on. He made out three figures standing around the front of an SUV with the hood up. Stilts signaled Candles.

Candles nodded and pressed a button on the phone display, pinging Rose. He started forward, gun in hand. Stilts, however, pressed his huge hand against the door.

"Hold up a sec. Let Rose get their attention, so we take them by surprise."

"That wasn't the plan, Stilts. What if Rose gets shot?"

"Then more money for the two of us."

Candles opened his mouth to protest but a cry and two shots stopped him. Stilts grinned and threw the door open to charge inside. Candles followed.

A brief gun battle ensued. The three men in the garage had drawn weapons and were firing into the rear of the garage, their backs to Stilts and Candles. They had no chance as Stilts and Candles opened fire. They were down in seconds.

"Make sure they are dead." Stilts started to say as he began to walk towards the office. "I'll look for the cash and the drugs-oh shit."

Candles looked up from one of the dead men he had shot in the back and followed Stilts' gaze. Rose was sitting against the rear wall near the back door, bleeding.

Stilts got to him first. He kneeled next to Rose and with his switchblade cut away some of his shirt. "Looks like a flesh wound, but there is a lot of blood."

"How you feeling man?" Candles asked, peering over Stilts' shoulder.

"I'm okay. Bullet just grazed me." Rose said weakly.

Candles saw a first aid cabinet on the wall behind the garage's service counter. He jogged over and rummaged through it, pulling out gauze and antiseptic. Stilts took them from him when he returned.

"I will take care of this." He told Candles. "You go check the office for the stash."

Candles went back to a small enclosed area behind the service counter. On a desk were two open duffle bags, one containing cash and the other with several packets of cocaine wrapped in plastic.

He grinned as he headed back out to the main garage with the bags. "Hey guys, the stash is here! Looks like we scored big time…"

Rose was not moving. Stilts knelt over him, his mouth close to his ear. As Candles rushed over, he realized Rose wasn't breathing, and saw Stilts' switchblade on the ground. It had more blood on it then when Stilts cut away Rose's shirt.

"I'm sorry man." Stilts said without looking up at Candles. "The bullet must have hit an artery and he bled out."

Candles tossed the money and drugs away.

176

"Jake Terrance." Candles whispered as he stood behind Stilts.

"What?"

"Jake Terrance." Candles whispered again as he pressed his gun to the back to Stilts' head. "That's my real name."

"WHY WOULD ANYONE PUT SOMETHING IN THERE?"

By Duanne Walton

A Halloween Pinata! Who knew?

My step-daughter threw a Halloween party and invited all her classmates.

We scoured Wal-Mart for themed party games.

And there it was - a black cat pinata.

And guess where the hole to put the candy in was!

So while I supervised a pack of running, shrieking grade-schoolers, my so-called wife stuffed candy into a cat's rear in the bedroom.

I explained the dire situation about the cat's anal intrusion and the kids sympathized. The cat needed shock therapy. And what could be more shocking than having kids take long sticks and beat the candy out of you?

The deed was done, and the cat was put out of its suffering. And so were we as the party ended. My step-daughter and some of her friends watched Jaws with an octopus with me while waiting for their parents. They actually cheered as the octopus dragged a baby into the water, stroller and all, as I screamed, "*That's it! You're going down, Calamari!*"

I can handle a lot of things in a horror movie but babies in jeopardy isn't one of them!

Sometime later, my so-called wife and step-daughter went on an emergency visit and I had the house to myself. I watched "Deliverance" for the first time.

Ned Beatty only *wished* he got candy shoved up his rear.

YOU ARE A SPRING DAY

By S. Houk

You are a spring day
on a bicycle
with the sun running before me

but behind three shorebirds
running ahead of me
not flying

then flying
each in turn turning
their white bellies to me
and then to the hot sun

not wondering what I'm doing
pedaling like a little girl
on my new little bike.

Biographies

Denise M. Baran-Unland is the author of the phantasmic BryonySeries.

This includes a supernatural/vampire trilogy for young and new adults and its five-volume prequel *Before the Blood*, the Adventures of Cornell Dyer chapter book series for grade school children and the Bertrand the Mouse series for young children.

Baran-Unland has six adult children, three adult stepchildren, fourteen total grandchildren, six godchildren, and four cats.

She is the co-founder of WriteOn Joliet and previously taught features writing for a homeschool coop, with the students' work published in the co-op magazine and The Herald-News in Joliet.

Baran-Unland blogs daily and is currently the features editor at The Herald-News. To read her feature stories, visit theherald-news.com.

To buy her books, read her blog, and follow her on social media, visit bryonyseries.com.

Holly Coop loves touching hearts with words. This genuine intent is evident in her inspirational poetry, motivational quotes, and spiritual insights. Holly has published three poetry collections
"A Cup of Inspiration to Go Please – My Heart Runneth Over", Heartstrings – Forever Wanderer", "Locks of Love – A Book of Encouragement, original and expanded edition, and coming soon - "A Line in the Sand – A Journey Towards Forgiveness".

In addition to poetry Holly also enjoys writing short stories, lyrics, and sharing thoughtful reflections and nuggets of wisdom on her blog, hollycoopauthor.wordpress.com.

She is a founding member of Romeoville Art Society, is employed as an office manager, and happily resides in Joliet with her husband, children, and furry friends.

Steven James Cordin has spent his entire life in Chicago and the South Suburbs. Cordin is a bank fraud and money laundering professional (Investigating, not committing).

A new member to WriteOn Joliet, his writing is in the area of fraud prevention, crime, and horror fiction. He currently lives alone near Joliet..

Jessica Harris was born in Chicago. She's lived across the U.S. and Europe and traveled extensively. She attended Trinity Christian College & Oxford University and graduated with a degree in history and education.

After beating cancer, she married her amazing husband in a castle (made complete with a groom-led archery shoot). She currently lives in Florida with her husband and their Newfoundland Dublin.

She's written multiple novel-length works and numerous short stories, and has been published in various anthologies.

Tom Hernandez is a writer, public speaker, performer and communications professional.

Born and raised in Joliet, Illinois, Hernandez has been writing personally and professionally since childhood.

His writing explores the many complicated facets of life — marriage, family, relationships, identity, aging, parenting, faith, social justice and politics.

He and his wife, Kellie have two adult daughters and welcomed their first grandchild in 2018. They live in Plainfield, Illinois. For more information, visit tomhernandezbooks.com.

S. Houk is a poet, awarding-winning playwright, and sound artist. Her work has appeared at Rhino fest in Chicago and the Emerging Playwrights Festival in Joliet, Illinois.

She is also a painter and photographer whose 2019 show in Joliet was titled: "Math & Nature".

When not writing, Houk does IT work, teaches at Lewis University, and walks in the forest.

Houk lives in Joliet with her imaginary Irish wolfhounds.

For more information, visit Sharonhouk.blogspot.com .

Lindsay Lake is a registered nurse with a degree in psychology. She's worked with mentally ill adults, teens and children.

Born in Ohio, she has lived in the Midwest, except for a 15-year stint in California for college at Shasta College and Sacramento State University. Governor State University is her alma mater.

She started writing at age ten. An avid film buff even then, she rewrote movies, saying they weren't quite right, and she needed to make them perfect. In adolescence she wrote short stories, poems and lyrics for an all-girl rock band.

Lake published a fanzine for ten years doing editing, writing, photography, layouts, plus interviews, and she toured with a rock band.

She has written three lengthy Avengers fanfiction novels published on archivesofourown.org.

As a nurse she studied all body parts and functioning, but none were so interesting to her as the human brain and human behavior. Her characters are flawed and full of psychic maladaptation. As a feminist she writes to liberate her male characters from toxic masculinity; for only then will the earth be free of aggression and war.

Recently Lake finished an adventure/romance/science fiction novel set in 1969 on Thule Air Force Base Greenland. Soon to be published somewhere.

She lives in Illinois, temporarily.

James Moore shares his biblically-centered perspective in articles, essays and poetry posted at brotherjames@writing.com and the Hub Pages online writing community.

He also has entrepreneurial "how to" articles included on toughnickel.com, a web site focused on how to earn, grow and save money.

Currently, Moore is building his budding publishing venture: Literary Jim Productions.

James Pressler is career analyst who has lived a double life for the past two decades as a creative writer, exploring the world beyond facts and figures.

His writing comes from a personal passion for storytelling, for offering new perspectives to familiar themes, with moods ranging from friendly humor to serious observations on the darker aspects of life.

Short stories and character sketches have been a compulsion for several years, and several stories have since been published, The first published novel was "The Book of Cain,"with two other manuscripts now being shopped.

For more information, visit writingandtheprocess.com.

Colleen H. Robbins has been writing since age 9, and has published everything from poems and stories to essays and novels. She prefers to write science fiction, fantasy, and horror, and loves to blend real science and mythological research into her stories when she can.

The third novel in her Daraga series, "Dark Protector," and her second short story collection, "Night Breeze and Moonbeams," should be out before the end of 2020. She currently lives in Illinois.

Duanne Walton said, "Writing is my gift from God and it's been with me forever. It's seen me through rough times and brought me to WriteOn Joliet where I've found support, encouragement and friends.

"I've also discovered other talents as an intrepid videographer, interpretive dancer (or mime), and comic strip writer/artist. I am blessed and thankful."

Katie Ward has worn many hats: teacher of the deaf, ballet teacher, choreographer, storyteller, wife, mother, and grandmother.

Now she hopes to try on a new hat, one that might fit a hopeful essayist who will help spouses of Alzheimer's patients navigate the murky waters that are their lives.

www.ingramcontent.com/pod-product-compliance
Lightning Source LLC
Chambersburg PA
CBHW022153260626
47155CB00018B/1865